Mangoes for Monkeys

A Novel By

Radhika Vyas Sharma

FROG BOOKS

ISBN 978-93-52010-84-4
Copyright © Radhika Vyas Sharma, 2018

First published in India in 2018 by Frog Books
An imprint of Leadstart Publishing Pvt. Ltd.

Sales Office:
Unit No. 25, Building No. A/1,
Near Wadala RTO,
Wadala (East), Mumbai – 400037, India
Phone: +91 96 99933000
Email: info@leadstartcorp.com
www.leadstartcorp.com

Editor: Kavya Shree
Cover: Dhiraj Navlakhe
Layouts: Ashwini Jadhav

For Dadaji.

Genealogy Chart

Daddyji – Sarojini

/

Suchitra – JP / Suchitra – Swayam

/

Geeta – Ajit

✳

Sahib Ram – Neti

/

Ram Sharan – Meena

Disclaimer

This is a work of fiction. Names, characters, businesses, places and events are either the product of author's imagination or are used in a fictitious manner. Therefore, any resemblance to real persons, living or dead is to be considered purely coincidental. All historical events mentioned in the book have been used fictitiously. It is not the intent of the author to offend any group, community, culture, religion, race, beliefs or social group.

Contents

About the Author

Radhika Vyas Sharma is the author of Parikrama: a collection of short stories and is currently at work on a novel. Radhika received her MFA in Creative Writing from the San Francisco State University. Notable honors include a teaching assistantship at San Francisco State University, a stint as Assistant Fiction Editor at 14 Hills: San Francisco State Graduate Literary Journal. Postgraduate work includes VONA: Voices of our Nation Foundation Workshops at UC Berkeley and Vermont Post Graduate Writer's Conference.

Radhika's writing credits include reviews and features for The San Francisco Chronicle, The San Jose Mercury News, The Times of India, The

Economic Times, KQED FM's Forum, Pacific Time and Perspectives, India Currents and several others: A short story Daddy Cool was featured in The Santa Clara Review, Spring 2010. Another story, Just a Photograph was showcased by Kearny Street Workshop in APAture 2013: Window into the work of Emerging Asian Pacific Artists.

1

Beautiful

Suchitra thought she looked beautiful when she cried. There was no way to tell but Suchitra was quite sure of it. Yet no one had photographed her in tears, not one time in Suchitra's seventy-six years.

"Why didn't you photograph me when I cried?" she had teased Swayam during a playful chat.

"You didn't cry enough," Swayam had said when she told him close to the end. His voice was still clear, only the bandage on his head a reminder of why they were in a hospital room.

"Nobody is going to be as interested in me as you."

"Don't be so sure."

With those last words Swayam was gone. Suchitra wanted to tell him, Wake up! These are terrible last words but she had trained herself to not waste energy on things that could not be changed so she did the pragmatic thing and buzzed for the nurse and the doctor. Suchitra cried in the privacy of her home for the next few months. After all, who is to console you when you lose the person who consoles you on all your losses?

Four years later, Suchitra would discover that as always, Swayam had been right. When Jon showed up at her Shimla doorstep Suchitra was secretly flattered. Suchitra liked artists with a hunger to learn. Suddenly she cared about how she looked. Sunken cheeks, drowning lungs, slowly becoming immobile legs—would the shadow of these not frighten Jon? And still she feigned disinterest.

Suchitra was in a contemplative state of mind the day Jon arrived seeking an audience with her. She typed him this single line on her laptop, this screen Meena—Ram Sharan's wife and now her de-facto nurse~caretaker—would turn in Jon's direction once the last key had been pressed.

Jon spoke softly, sitting hunched in the little chair by the side of the window; he was not particularly cogent, but his voice had the urgency that younger artists display in front of older, more accomplished artists. It does not matter what their words be for all they want to say is: Trust me for we speak the same language.

Jon spoke with the fearlessness of a man who has lost everything. An urgent, fearless man. How can such a man, this man who is no longer ducking pain and humiliation, fail if he sets his mind to something? Even if that something be the intention to watch a reclusive 80-year-old die. Such a man cannot be denied because for him now the world is a dewdrop on a leaf, waiting to fall on the ground. But he is not waiting, he is no longer held captive by his thirst.

Just then a man about Suchitra's age, more vital than her save for his slight stoop, entered the room. Seeing this man, her father-in-law, Meena covered her head with the pallav of her sari which she'd carelessly let drop to her shoulders while taking care of Suchitra.

He fixed his eyes on Jon. "Young man," he spoke in an odd mixture of British and Indian accents, "I'm afraid you are tiring her."

Jon had come ready to fail, yet he could not bring himself to leave. And sometimes success or failure is simply a matter of waiting it out. Luckily for Jon, a five-minute silence was enough to make a dent in Suchitra's heart.

Jon stood up to leave.

"Wait, Jon," said Suchitra. With her eyes still closed, she whispered, "What do you want?"

"Just to hang around."

Suchitra and Sahib Ram looked at each other.

"The doctor has asked Babyji to rest," said Sahib Ram. Jon nodded.

Suchitra let Jon stay. To hang around, to film her dying, or at least close to it. Jon looked no older than thirty, so Suchitra guessed he'd be around thirty-five—time does not maul men like it does women, at least at the beginning of the race.

Before Meena and Sahib Ram ushered Jon out to the guest room, Suchitra typed her last sentence.

What will you film as I get closer?

Suchitra's fingers fell limp soon after but the voice and her mind appeared just the same.

"Not you, something else maybe," said Jon, a little surprised at the turn of events. Fifteen minutes ago they were debating whether to keep him or send him back and now Suchitra was asking him this question. He wanted to make something light of it, say something like, wow, I've earned my subject's trust pretty quickly, but he knew this thing that had happened to him, he had not earned it. And Sahib Ram was glaring at him. Jon offered a brief smile and made way to his room.

That one nod from Suchitra changed the newly coalesced structure of Carmen Hall. Sahib Ram stayed back after Meena and Jon had left.

"Sahib Ram, I can move my arm today," Suchitra said with amazement in her voice. She could sense that Sahib Ram was still angry. "He has come to me...to learn, to learn how to experiment, to learn how to play with his camera. Let him stay,

Sahib Ram." Sahib Ram remained silent. Suchitra knew the meaning of Sahib Ram's silences.

"I know the meaning of your silence, Sahib Ram," said Suchitra, out loud this time.

Jon's arrival would have been a moment of celebration had he arrived when Suchitra was in good health. But Suchitra had only been back in Carmen Hall for ten days and in rapidly failing health. Both Sahib Ram and Suchitra were aware of the circumstances. Nevertheless, Suchitra being the one who had cemented Jon's stay felt duty bound to appear easy about it.

The idea of a return to Shimla had come to Suchitra on a good health day after several bad nights. Everything had become harder after Swayam passed. So, whenever she had a good day she seized it—did things with it. One such a day presented itself three weeks ago. On the 16th of January 2000.

Suchitra had called a different place home on that day, her home in Bay Hills, the home that would pass on to her second child, her daughter

Maya. A day that had arrived after several nights of waking up in cold fits and weeks of sleeplessness for Suchitra, Maya and her always dependable nurse, Marge. A good day; a present after five 911 calls in eight weeks. On such days Suchitra could still walk—to the restroom and back. For showers too. She could sit straight for meals. Living was still not too bad.

That morning Marge had only just seated her on her shower seat. They had decided that today they would allow her hair to get wet. Suchitra closed her eyes, and instead of the auburn-black greeness that she saw every day, she saw other things. They didn't flash in front of her eyes and fade away like the images from previous days. This time the images, they lingered, going back and forth between themselves. Over and over, she saw them: her monkeys, her bench, her painter sitting on the bench, his nose in a book, his hair covered by a newsboy cap, Daddyji, Bui, Ajit sobbing and falling after delivering his Swayam 'Swayam'—a man for all seasons speech and he will stay that way till Geeta and Maya go pick him up and fold him into themselves, Suchitra still not crying, the home empty without Swayam and his gentle silence, her body as it used to be—taut, fat, slim, limp, soft... She opens her eyes, now she sees Daddyji, his rages, his failing eyesight, Daddyji kissing baby Ajit on the forehead, Bui looking out at the mountains, Sahib Ram wearing his Sunday market tweeds, Suchitra, sixteen, dancing and dancing, the carpet inching and sliding up the wall as she dances, her very own ditty to the tune of bum bum dabumm bumm bumm.

He's so nice. So very nice. So so nice. So so very. Very very very.

He's my nice. My mine. All mine. All mine.

And then the monkeys, her monkeys, waiting, smiling, waiting.

That is when Suchitra knew that death was standing somewhere near. It looked like it could wait patiently for a little bit, but she knew that it would soon get fidgety. She needed to move quickly. Suchitra summons for Maya, who, newly divorced and irritable, came running from her Sacramento office. But Maya cannot handle Suchitra alone. She needs an ally and now that her father is gone, it has to be her half-brother Ajit, ten years her senior. He listens on speaker phone from London as the women argue between themselves.

"Mother, I need to close this deal before I can fly back. We need to wait if I have to take you to Shimla."

"Who said you have to take me?" Suchitra, annoyed.

Ajit, ever the tactician, is quick with his volley. "Mother, the Y2K concern for airplanes has still not been resolved, and I would rather we not be the ones to find out first hand."

"I'm not bonkers, Ajit! I saw on TV; nothing happened on the 1st of January. All the planes are flying just fine!" Suchitra was coughing from the force of the exertion. Suchitra often neglected her health to make her point but it came with a price, of course.

Ajit laughed softly but didn't respond to her outburst and asked to speak to Maya privately instead. And that was that. From that moment onwards, everything moved fast, incredibly fast.

Once they'd booked the tickets they called Carmen Hall. Sahib Ram answered the phone.

"Kaise ho, Sahib Ram?"

Recognizing her voice immediately, Sahib Ram replied, "Babyji," and then he became quiet, overcome by the moment, overcome by the sound of Suchitra's voice.

Suchitra felt a sharp pain around her right shoulder. Unused to silences over the telephone, Suchitra spoke for the both of them.

"Sahib Ram, I am well, Sahib Ram. I want to come home, Sahib Ram. May I return to Carmen Hall, Sahib Ram?"

"This has always been your home, Babyji," he said. "My son will come to fetch you from the airport." Another long pause, "I will wait for you at home, Babyji."

Packing was not difficult; Maya and her daughter Trisa came to help Suchitra pack. Suchitra had many things in her home but had spent much of her last half decade inscribing the initials of the names of her three children and four grandchildren under the base of each figurine, on the tags of sateen or cotton sheets or stuffing them in boxes with distinct names on it. It did not matter that one of her children had been a stillborn. After Suchitra would die, Maya would take the box with her biological brother's name on it and take her time to decide where and what should be donated. A lifetime of losses had prepared Suchitra well for dying.

Suchitra and Maya had thought that it would have been easier to convince their nurse Marge to accompany Suchitra to India than get Ajit's approval; they were both a little surprised when he did not demur much. The nurse though blanched at the idea of travelling to India, and it was therefore left to Ajit to take Suchitra to New Delhi. But New Delhi was as far as Ajit could go for a little while. He had business to do in New Delhi. So, it would be Ram Sharan, Sahib Ram's son, who would take Suchitra to Carmen Hall in Shimla, leaving Ajit to wind up and join Suchitra soon and for as long as he was needed. Ajit thought that this would prove itself to be a satisfactory final offering to his mother.

As Ajit started wheeling Suchitra towards security, Maya placed Suchitra's Nikon F3 camera in her lap; Suchitra's longest running camera, Suchitra's most celebrated work emerging from its innards. Suchitra, suddenly perky now that she was out of the home and away from Marge's well-intentioned restrictions, said, "Why take the flute when it cannot be played?"

"Hang around your flute mother. Give your restlessness to someone else," Maya said kissing Suchitra on the cheek, trying hard not to cry. As their flight took off, Suchitra closed her eyes and thought, You get your wish, Sahib Ram. I return to you, Sahib Ram.

✳ ✳ ✳

2

Carmen Hall

When Suchitra decided to come to Carmen Hall, they started putting photographs of her all over the home—on dressers, bookcases, other high places save the three rooms that had been kept separate as holiday rentals *(Let the house pay for itself, Babyji,* Sahib Ram had said thirty-seven years ago, long before it became fashionable to have houses pay for themselves). One look at Carmen Hall and you knew that the home belonged to Suchitra, or at least wanted to belong to her. Suchitra as a young girl in pigtails, Suchitra with Daddyji, Baby Suchitra with Bui and Ma Sarojini. Of course, the maximum photographs were those of Suchitra with Ajit, her first born. Sahib Ram choose to place all the photographs that Suchitra had sent to him sporadically over the past four decades on the mantel near the drawing room fire place. Suchitra with as-tall-as-her Ajit and baby Maya, Suchitra with an angry-faced Maya and a very tall Ajit. Swayam was nowhere to be seen in most of the pictures for Swayam was the guy pressing the click button. All these photographs set in place to make Suchitra happy, so she may feel welcome in her own home.

But Suchitra was raging inside the moment she entered Carmen Hall. There was no expansion in her chest, the kind you feel when you enter a big home, especially if that home happens to be yours. Her body had not taken the winding roads well; she felt nauseated and suffocated. Suchitra wanted so much to say that everything looks the same but it didn't. So many new hotels, so many old buildings razed, gone. Instead, in their places stood multi-storied concrete structures, jostling with advertisements on large display boards, all precariously placed on hilltops, fighting a battle they were destined to lose with the Indian dust. The only consolation had been to be able to see the city one time in the morning. It was good to be reminded that everything had changed. Only the things those places had done to her remained the same. Throughout her ride from Kalka to Shimla, Suchitra wished she had not waited this long to return to Carmen Hall. She wanted to halt. Take photographs. Ride the small, gentle train, fondly nicknamed the 'toy train'. Once she had savored its slowness with JP. Her John Papi. At least that time he was hers. Or so it appeared.

Then she remembered why she was going to Shimla—to die. So now, no more photographs. Only the eye, and the moment. And then the nausea and the suffocation hit her again. Knocked her hard and the cold, cold body, not solely because of the weather. The weather was as it should have been: cold, chilly, accompanied by denuded trees and slippery streets but the mountain sides looked dry, desiccated. *What happened to the snow this year? Did we not get enough? Why am I gasping so much? I'm a mountain girl!* The nurse who had joined her from Delhi, Rekha, held her hand tight and asked Ram Sharan to drive, slowly, slowly, and he tried, but there was only so much he could do on a single lane highway. Despite their best efforts, despite the heating in the Rover Jeep, the cold air kept seeping through and into the vehicle, sapping Suchitra's energy.

At each step of journey, in Hong Kong, in New Delhi, in Kalka, Suchitra told herself that it would get better when she reached Carmen Hall. But one look at Carmen Hall and she knew who was to blame. *Ajit.* Ajit had phoned and changed everything. New rugs, new sofa, new, new, new. This rage melted the moment she saw the sheet on the large size hospital style adjustable bed that was now to be hers. Soft blue and pink cotton with little petals and leaves. This is what she had come here for. A pillow and sheet both soft and cold, to absorb the heat of living. Suchitra had not been denied that.

This was the home where both Daddyji and her aunt, Bui, had died. Not the sanatorium that had claimed Ma Sarojini or the hospitals that would bring to rest JP and Swayam. The last three places were out of reach for Suchitra. Then there was her window. The window from which she'd spied JP coming to meet Daddyji. To ask for her. That same window. In this very room. That same JP who would one day send her Swayam. This room would be close enough to all of them. And then of course, she found the monkeys outside the next day. And suddenly everything started to make sense.

❋

Just the day after Jon's arrival, the water began to thaw in the taps. Meena, Carmen Hall's caretaker and Sahib Ram's daughter-in-law, loved the feel of freely flowing tap water on her fingers; nothing like easy water to make her dirty dishes clean, never mind what it did to her fingers afterward. Her husband, Ram Sharan, Sahib Ram's son, had returned from New Delhi after a weekend trip the same morning. Meena filled him in with the events of the past day. Ram Sharan's jaw hardened as Meena's story drew to a close. A gora boy to take pictures of a dying woman, very nice.

"*Poora tamasha banaye hai,*" he said spitting a little of the chai Meena had put in front of him. "Aur yeh kitni kaali kaali chai hai!"

Meena bit her lip and apologized for the excessively black tea. She had nothing to say about the spectacle part. She couldn't help but agree with her husband, yet she liked this new American who had entered their lives. Jon—gentle, not so tall, nervous, edgy but attractive in an oblique way. Irresistible like a child; oblivious to his own magnetism just like a child. But Meena did not want to let her husband in on her feelings. To have Ram Sharan believe that she mirrored his minutest thoughts had been her perpetual quest since the day they had been married almost three and a half decades ago.

"So what is this? Do all big creatives die like this? With someone filming them?" Meena—she'd meant for it to be a whisper but the flowing tap and her nervous energy made her pitch and tone stronger, almost strident—said. Her husband, Sahib Ram's only child, shushed her, this time even more irritably than he was want to do. He'd spotted Jon in the corridor. Now Jon was opening the refrigerator. Now he was staring intently at the contents of the refrigerator. Now he had made his choice. Jon did not understand Hindi, although he had made a mental note to change that ever since his train ride from Kalka to Shimla grand station. Red Bull in hand, Jon walked away. Plonked himself on the sofa outside Suchitra's room. Legs wide apart, back straight. Eyes closed. Twenty minutes later he was up and un-zipping black duffel handbags, blowing the dust off camera lenses, wiping their mist covered lenses with a soft white cloth, unlocking tripods. One, two, three. One camera on tripod. The other two hung around his neck. Jon was firing his coals. It was contagious. Ram Sharan and Meena got to work too. Meena with cleaning and prepping, Ram Sharan with planning and phoning.

Curiously, the presence of the camera made

Ram Sharan resist Jon a little less, even though he would never admit as much to his wife. Within a few days, Jon would become a member of this motley household; in a snap, just like that. And this, simply because he had been allowed to set his things down.

From her raised bed, Suchitra could see Jon set himself up. When he was all done, she felt incredibly light, almost revived by the ease that comes about from a decision rightly taken. But then the sinking feeling in her lungs returned. Suchitra started wheezing, but motioned Jon to keep working. It was almost as if everything had been set in place for Jon to arrive and start filming. Jon got to work fast. He took off his jacket, even though it was cold and he could feel it. Jon liked to shiver. It made him feel alive.

Suchitra's room was the best lit in the house. A skylight from the roof shone sunlight and moonlight, a door connected it to the outside world, and then there was her window. Her favorite place in the whole world. Suchitra was half-afraid Jon would interrupt her looking out of the window. But Jon quickly made himself unobtrusive. Suchitra loved looking at the monkeys. They'd arrived a day before Jon and Jon had arrived just in time. The arrival of the monkeys at this time of the year surprised Meena and Ram Sharan; Sahib Ram, though, said nothing. Nothing surprised Sahib Ram in life. He just came and stood beside Suchitra's bed with his slight hunch in his heavy Khadi Gram Udyog black overcoat, blue trousers and green Kangra cap from time to time. After all, Ajit had entrusted his mother to him. Nothing could go wrong till Ajit arrived. And then, they would wait for it together. Suchitra awoke whenever Sahib Ram was by her side—mostly it looked like she was sleeping, but who knew whether she was sleeping or simply had her eyes closed.

"Sahib Ram," she said, her breathing shallow, labored and loud enough for Sahib Ram to hear, "I have these vivid dreams from our childhood days."

Sahib Ram looked at her attentively, anticipating a question about her condition. He was both right and wrong about Suchitra.

"What does it mean if I can only remember,

can only think about my childhood?" Suchitra continued.

To which Sahib Ram said to no one in particular, "Arre, bahar kitne bandar hain?" *How many monkeys are outside the window?* As many as needed for Suchitra. The idea of the promise returned to her.

The monkeys were her favorite part of the day. Yesterday Suchitra had spotted a little baby monkey in that group. If Suchitra raised her bed and Meena propped her pillows, she could see them fairly well. The monkeys were energetic. It was a small troop. Mocha khaki skins with red faces. But it pinched to be in that raised position all the time. Suchitra wished she could see more, but her body was winding down and she had to constantly remind herself that it was a body that served her well for so long and now if it sought rest, she must not begrudge it. Still the feeling returned when she would see the monkeys jump across the trees; she wanted to get up from this bed which held her captive, and look at them, watch them love, hate, live, much like Jon was doing to her in that very room. Memory was

Suchitra's only consolation. She beckoned it often and it never failed her, served her dutifully. Suchitra focused her thoughts on the last time she'd seen a monkey infant.

Ajit arrived a few days after Jon's arrival. Meena cooked food specially for Ajit the morning he arrived—split chick peas in tight gravy and halwa. Ajit flew to the Asia Pacific six times a year but never quite got used to the long flight times. Business class did nothing to dull his resentment. Still, he was good with keeping things under wraps.

Upon arrival, Ajit immediately took a dislike to Sahib Ram's son, who was unloading his bags, without any apparent reason. Jon's presence he resented but did not dislike as much. Ajit stared at Ram Sharan for a bit, taking in his cocky manner, his surly skin, his tobacco chewing ways, his two broken front teeth. Ajit could not fathom how such a man could be Sahib Ram's son. But Sahib Ram, Sahib Ram he trusted; the affection from his childhood days now transformed into a quiet regard. Then one taste of Meena's halwa and Ajit realized that he had become his mother. Jon came back that afternoon to report to Suchitra that there was a young monkey in the group. Suchitra had been right. She wanted to visit the monkey troop, but that was no longer possible, so she closed her eyes and found a memory.

3
Monkeys, Circa 1938

Everything is choppy for now, for Suchitra in this life that is hers now. Only memories are seamless, safe, sound and full.

Suchitra has known JP for a year now. This year Suchitra is head girl at the convent. The nuns are not happy about it. No one wants a head girl who just wants to be happy. No, they want a head girl who wants to be a lady. But an election is an election and Suchitra has earned her place.

JP and Suchitra are on a small off-shoot of the Mall Road. If you asked anyone what the name of this road is, they would look askance and say, "The Mall Road, of course." Only JP knows the truth and he will share it with Suchitra the first week they met. That seems like a long time ago to JP but only yesterday to Suchitra.

This day, this May day, the trees have stopped shedding cones with the ferocity they displayed a few months ago. They are sitting on their bench. No really, it's just JP, John Papi, the newly-returned-from-London son of her music teacher, Mrs. Andrews, who is sitting on their bench. The bench is on a bend in the road. Why it should be called a road when no horse or man drawn vehicles are allowed on it remains a mystery to Suchitra. At a little farther distance from the bend, sits Nanga Baba wearing nothing save a thick *khal* loincloth and matted hair. He sits there with his parrot and lots of little cards. Cards to help you learn about yourself, your future. But JP, JP is an artist, and an artist is the future. JP knows all he needs to know about himself; he has no use for those cards. And when JP is by her side, Suchitra is interested in nothing else either. Suchitra knows that JP is her future, and today he is by her side. JP has this forget-about-the-future effect on women and while he knows of this phenomenon, he mostly chooses not to use it. Except for one exception. Even the normally suspicious nuns are lighter around perennially half-serious, half-jesting JP. When JP is around they are interested in art, in painting, in music too. JP is a little bit of a bad boy but around him they almost forget that they have sworn to be good girls.

There are monkeys all around them. JP sits with his newsboy cap drawn over his forehead, almost covering his eyes. He has his nose in a book. Suchitra cannot sit still. There are monkeys everywhere. She is not afraid of them anymore, the way she used to be when they first moved to Shimla a decade ago, after her mother died. Or rather, because Suchitra's mother died.

Suchitra walks closer to them. The monkeys act like they don't care. But when Suchitra draws closer to the little ones, that is when they act sharp. They make noises; their brown, dark-earth bodies now in battle mode, their red faces taut and fierce with tension.

Suchitra backs off. They are licking and eating the *guthli* of a fresh mango. Someone has had a feast of mangoes, someone is well in the world and is celebrating—the mangoes being the leftover of that celebration. The monkeys—they nibble, suck, slurp on the hard core; there is enough mango pulp around the seed of the fruit, enough to tantalize a monkey. Suchitra surmises that the *guthli* was either thrown away by careless feasting lovers or by a rich person stealing an afternoon with himself, away from the demands of his entourage. Young Suchitra can only surmise for she does not know of anyone who will throw away the core with so much mango flesh still stuck on it.

Suddenly Suchitra wants mangoes too. She doesn't care how they are served to her. Who cares if it's in the form of the elegant and liquidy aamras like Bui—her aunt—makes in the summers for her brother, Suchitra's Daddyji, or if it was a mango-chikoo fruit salad, a Sahib Ram invention, mixing two things that were not usually mixed but very tasty nonetheless, or messy mango pulp on hands, face and cheeks and a satisfied smile on the face—her very own Suchitra signature. Suchitra wants to ask JP how he likes his mangoes but before that, she asks the monkeys.

"Kya re, bandar? Which fruit would you like to enjoy? A *meetha-meetha* mango? Maybe oranges...?"

"Tomorrow, I will bring you many, many mangoes and while all of you eat, I will watch."

The young monkey looks at Suchitra from the safety of its mother's embrace with a smile, almost like he understands, anticipating the delight of the fruit promised to this monkey troop.

But that tomorrow that Suchitra has imagined will not manifest, at least not yet. In about fifteen minutes after Suchitra has made her way back to the bench and caught her breath, JP will ask Suchitra to marry him. JP has received a scholarship. He is to sail to London again. He shows her the official letter, kisses her lightly on the cheek. Left cheek. Suchitra will feel a surge around her heart. Suchitra thinks first, *What is this? Why did I have to be in school uniform at this moment?* and then she says yes, because no would not have been the correct answer. Tomorrow they will meet Daddyji. Together. For the first time. And then, one week later, three days before she will sail, Daddyji will slap her on the cheek. Right cheek. A harsh touch on the cheek that will go straight to Suchitra's heart.

JP has already started walking back towards the church, towards the library at the crown of the Mall Road. He walks in big strides and it feels as if an invisible force is propping him forward and pushing him. Suchitra hangs back, just for a bit longer to look at her monkeys. Within the past twenty minutes Suchitra has made two promises that will swallow the rest of her life.

JP, he is tall, but he is so limber, he looks taller because of it. His hair is parted in the center, soft brown hair, brown eyes. He stops, turns, folds his arms across his chest. Suchitra can no longer linger and makes her way towards him.

In the years that went by, Suchitra did not forget about her promise. The monkeys beckoned her everyone. In labor rooms. On ocean waters. Through camera lenses. Inside dark room filters. Then why did she not carry it out, *her promise,* earlier? Why didn't she carry it out when she lived in a better body? Why didn't she carry it out to those very same monkeys, or perhaps their descendants, on the two occasions that she came back to Shimla after she'd first sailed away on *The Pioneer?* No, it would not have been possible sooner.

It was not just mangoes that she'd promised. It was also the quality of the heart that had promised those mangoes. That quality, that lightness of heart had been compromised the day JP walked away, leaving her and Ajit in that derelict and messy but alive, throbbing until yesterday but now only empty, lonely apartment on Earls Court, and ten quid for baby Ajit on the dresser. Suchitra's heart never recovered from having to send a telegram to Bui the next morning.

Suchitra's monkeys are all dead now. Young Suchitra is dead too. Only the sun that watched them is still alive. Yes, it was a younger sun, but still alive. Old Suchitra is still alive too, breathing despite the fluid in her lungs. Much has changed. The only thing that remains unchanged is the name. They were called monkeys when dead and monkeys when alive. Suchitra when young and Suchitra when old. In this quality they rival God. The merciful god. The careful god. But always, god.

After 62 years, an old Suchitra wants to give these new monkeys mangoes which were once promised to dead monkeys under a much younger sun.

✳ ✳ ✳

4

Suchitra, Carmen Hall, Circa 2000

I know why it had to be Carmen Hall and not the home Swayam and I built together. When I touch my face, my body, everything about me is soft. It is not the plump softness of youth, but it is the gooey, desiccated softness of a fruit returning to its tree. What is the use of old, saggy skin? Swayam would have laughed had I posed him this question.

I once loved and lived under the shade of someone adroit at using sagging skin. Bui, my aunt, would flatten mango skins, rubbing them against the walls of her wide bottomed silver bowl, massaging the last ounce of sweetness from them. Bui would impress upon me the importance of not letting even an atom of sweetness get lost. I am seven. I would think about what Bui has just said. Then, my inevitable question: Did my mother cook like this too, Bui? No, Bui says, she was freer in the world. "Let it go to the earth, Aradhana," she would tell my Bui. "Nothing is ever lost. The earth needs its sweetness back."

"I think your mother was a little bit of a poetess, Suchitra." Bui and my mother were close friends.

I am now an empty husk. Now what? Just the mind. The mind is my camera, the eyes its lens. Its focus. But also, long as there is breath, there is desire; you fulfill one and another arises in its place. I think I must come to Shimla to be close to those who love me, to the beginning, now that the end is near. This wish has been fulfilled. Then I think I want to see the monkeys. I want to walk to my childhood vista points.

And suddenly this young man shows up. To become my eyes. This young man who reminds me of my JP—the way he holds his feelings so tight and so loose, the way he looks at me, this urgency to learn to paint pictures with his camera. He is so much like my painter. My JP. My John Papi. I want so much to utter his name with my tongue. But I cannot say his name because Ajit has grieved enough.

So many years I have spent trying to forget, railing against that moment when he said to me what all he did. Then comes next morning and he is gone.

All the canvasses, the colors, all gone. Everything drenched from my life. From Ajit's life. But now is the time to forgive. Time to remember JP's love. Remember how we made Ajit. On that ship right away — we lost no time.

It was a fairy tale-to-be on the ship. The Pioneer. It was a young ship; when you are young everyone wants to be a pioneer, even ships. We got busy when we reached ashore. He, with his canvas, paints and brushes. Me, with the typing, the dictation, the writing and the wiring. We were happy. I thought he was happy. What happened? Ajit happened. Those naked models. The nappies, the bottles, the clothes, my stained garments on the bathroom floor. They all jostled for space with his colours, his paints. Why did he fear them? Were they that powerful? What did he have that he was afraid to lose? Or did he just want to lose and then no longer be afraid? He says to me, "I am leaving you, Suchitra. Whatever you want in life, I will get for you, always. But I cannot stay." I open my mouth to say something, to tell him, I left everything for you, now what is left for me? but when his eyes catch mine I immediately realize the uselessness of it. I am the daughter of a disciplined man. I am, above all, schooled in the importance of usefulness. JP has been my only indulgence. Ajit cries as his little speech is over.

Ajit cries and these cries will not be muffled by the bottle I thrust in his infant mouth automatically. He pushes the bottle away. The loose nipple falls off the cylinder, the formula all over the green carpet. The land lady, Sheri, will not charge us for that formula or for ruining the red–black Persian carpet when I tell her. She will do what Ajit did when he heard of it—Sheri cried at the news that JP had abandoned me and Ajit.

Why do I not remember my Swayam as much? Why must I remember the man who promised me the world, gave me a taste and then took it all away? Why do I not remember the man who loved me with all my scars? Why am I so riveted by my scars?

In this boy, my painter comes to me another time. I am gasping for air but he is truly gasping. I asked him, "What do you think you can get from an old girl?" And he said, "The real thing." Yes, the real thing. This boy has come to me to be my eyes. Now that I have my eyes, I have another desire. My Ajit is here. Tomorrow I must ask him. Ask him to arrange for the monkeys the mangoes I had promised them. Before I leave.

There is much that I can say about death. There is a charge, a force to it, almost as if the room is caving into me and lifting me up at the same time. But there is one thing I will not and cannot tell anyone—that dying can sometimes be easy.

5
Asking

It is February 2000. This is the present moment. It is destined to become the past. It's only been four days since he arrived, but Jon has won Suchitra's confidence already. He brings Suchitra pictures of the young monkey, enlarged and uploaded on her laptop for Suchitra to view and savor. Jon's camera goes where the raised bed cannot.

The young monkey was a special one. Not simply because he was the only little one in the entire troop, no, there was something bright about him, something that told his elders that he was meant to be protected, so that one day he could protect several others.

From her bed Suchitra wondered what had happened to the other baby monkeys. It was little solace that even if she might have had the use of her legs, the answer to this question would not have become manifest immediately. Meena would tell her each morning as she sponged her and put on a fresh gown and socks followed by tucking her snugly in blankets, that she'd never seen monkeys outside this window, and especially at this time of the year, calling it an oddity. This was something Suchitra often meditated on. The monkeys were just like Suchitra—showing up unannounced, keeping everyone guessing about their intention.

Jon brought her new pictures while Meena tied her thin gray in a plait, straightening out the waves with a soft comb and finishing up by knotting two extra fine fabric scrunchies to hold the braided hair in place. Maya had stocked Suchitra well with soft scrunchies to prevent any scalp irritation and unnecessary hair loss.

"They look sprightly," Suchitra said when she finally had time for her laptop.

Jon smiled. "I didn't know their monkey backsides were red too."

Now it was Suchitra's turn to smile. A knowing one. "There is an eagle in the background," said Suchitra.

Jon nodded. Suchitra puckered her lips and

grew a few lines on her forehead.

When Ajit entered the room a few minutes later, Jon moved his chair to make room for him.

"I was wondering if you could do something for me, Ajit," she said.

"What is it, mother?" he looked at her intently, unsure of what to expect.

"Perhaps some mangoes for him?" said Suchitra, pointing to the picture of the monkey, a screensaver on her laptop.

6

Names

What's in a name! said Shakespeare.

Suchitra's Daddyji would say a rose by any other name would not be just as sweet. Ask Suchitra's parents, who named her after a Tagore heroine. Or even Suchitra herself—calling her aunt Bui instead of Buha; yes, yes, Suchitra is only 16 months old when she makes that decision, but we must remember that it was never challenged or amended. Many aunts are addressed as Buha, only Suchitra calls hers Bui. And mango? Who was it that decided to call a mango, *mango, aam?* What might have suggested itself to him or her? Was it because of its taste or the way it felt to touch? Or was it because of something it did to the tongue? Feel the words in your mouth as your teeth bite into soft, succulent mango flesh. Mango. Aam. *Aa* plus *mmm.* Every name a mystery, waiting to be unlocked.

But before we learn of names, we must learn of two men—of the homes they built, the lives they created, the hearts they broke, the hope they planted. Two men from humble beginnings: Daddyji and his right-hand man, Sahib Ram's father. They found each other in the trenches of Europe in WWI. They believed that they were valued and that belief kept them going. Their action a proof of their belief.

The better off between the two men was the son of a school teacher, his third son, the only son who would live beyond 35. No tuberculosis for him, thank you very much. He, this man who escaped tuberculosis, Daddyji, and his man Friday fought bravely. They didn't bring home any visible scars and looked good. The Robinson Crusoe between the two then found himself in Calcutta and his boss saw how he looked at his only daughter when she entered the room. Saw that this young man had made a wish in his heart. This man with a daughter, gave expression to his gratitude, gave this young man his only daughter, Sarojini. They would soon have a daughter and because of this daughter this young man would be known to those who knew him as Daddyji.

Man Friday was already married when he and Daddyji met in the trenches. He came home to his wife and she promptly gave him a son. When Daddyji came visiting his Man Friday's he tells them of his Suchitra born just a few months ago. He looks at the toddler son of his best friend and says, "You look like a Sahib, now what have you come to do?" The name stuck. Sahib Ram. Son of Ganga Ram. Almost son of Daddyji. No one remembers what Sahib Ram's original name might have been.

Daddyji's new life was perfect. Two women of his own and now a third one, his sister, joined him after their father passed away. Aradhana. Also known as Bui. Bui will then fall in love with a Captain when Suchitra is just a year old. They will meet, write letters, be brazen enough to pose for an open air photo together. And then Aradhana's brother will find out. He will rage, explode, cite several reasons. The day Aradhana decides to run away with the Captain, she will find out that her sister-in-law has tuberculosis. There is no escaping the fates after all. Sarojini will become pale, her husband's neglect imploding inside her and Man Friday and his family will come to her aid. Sarojini will die. The Captain will get a new posting. Aradhana will find out that she and the Captain will not have the luck of Fredrick Wentworth and Anne Elliot in Persuasion.

They will not get another chance.

Tuberculosis wins, Sarojini dies. It is a slap on the face for Daddyji. He becomes hot and cold. Mostly cold. Soft sometimes but only for Sahib Ram. *Sahib Ram must go to school. Sahib Ram must learn this, Sahib Ram must learn that. Sahib Ram, Sahib Ram, Sahib Ram...*

With Sarojini gone, Bui must take over. Must do what Sarojini would have done. It feels heavy, this role, almost like a petite woman wearing the jacket of a tall one. The sleeves, long and loose, the shoulders droopy, the length pulling you down; instead of enjoying its warmth, this cloak only reminds you of how now you must carry what was not made for you.

On days when her heart gets very heavy, Aradhana unlocks an old suitcase and looks at the sari that the Captain bought her, the same sari that she wore in that photograph, the sari she wore the evening the Captain was refused and refused not gently. She feels that the story of her life is like a sentence written, then erased. And then in that moment Suchitra will come and fold herself in her lap and Bui will cry softly. Suchitra, always ready to fight with Bui, will say nothing when Bui puts her in bed and then Bui's salty tears *drip, drip* over her forehead, down the widow's peak and to the bridge of her nose. That night, Bui decides that she will keep a little fire burning inside her. For Suchitra. To comfort Suchitra when Daddyji is cold. And Daddyji is mostly cold. Shimla is a cold place.

Five years after Suchitra's mother's death, Sahib Ram will also find himself motherless. *Doesn't matter,* he thinks to himself, *mother is in the heart and heart is in the books.* He is doing well at school and Daddyji is so proud of him. But when Sahib Ram sees his father stooping, the realization that his childhood is on its way out raises its ugly head.

Sahib Ram sees them huddling together around the fire more evenings than usual: Daddyji on his chair, Ganga Ram on the floor, crouched and folded into a ball, the heels of his feet touching the hips and his arms folded, hugging the knees close. It is hard to tell who is the master, who is the servant— the man who came into power, wealth and fortune but lost the unconditional love of his family or the man who will stick around and by just that make

Daddyji his slave.

They are sparring.

"He's my son," says Daddyji.

"If only, Sahib ji. Do not give him a cup when the world will not allow him to quench his thirst," says Ganga Ram. Daddyji is shaking his head. They cannot decide. Sahib Ram decides for them by bringing in a tray of chai for Daddyji. Sahib Ram has always been helping out Bui or Suchitra around the house but never Daddyji; only servants serve Daddyji and in that moment Daddyji feels as if someone has turned a knife in his heart and that no matter what he does in life he is doomed to fail.

All this while we've been talking only of Daddyji's family. Desertion and death is not their special privilege. Every family on earth gets a taste of this cake. In the same town and on the same Mall road, a few years before Suchitra, a baby boy is born to a couple not meant to be together but brought together by life. The woman, an English governess, the man, someone who was one thing one day, another thing another day. A man of varied heritage. This man, John Papi Sr, is a wanderer, but when little

John Papi arrives, he tries to rein in his impulses. He asks himself to stay content in the pines, for the sake of his young son. But he cannot do so for long. John Papi Sr was lured in to stay longer because of the beauty of the pine trees. The once governess, now a music teacher, feels orphaned a second time. This time without any hope of being rescued. She will snip *Junior* out of John Papi, her four year old son's name. She will sing the sweetest songs in the convent and year after year girls will leave her music class feeling speechless. And one day she will meet Suchitra and speak of her to her son, now a grown up with magic fingers and magic eyes.

"What's her name, mother?" he will ask her as she knits to relax in front of the fireplace.

She will look up. "Who?"

"That girl whom you said is so good with words and sings beautiful songs?"

For Suchitra it's all about words. When the right words come to express something: anger, contempt, even love, the day feels brighter. But often she does not have the words and she does not know what to do. So she knows intuitively that before she learns of the words, she must learn of the names. *Why do we call anything by its special name?* Suchitra is a good student. She learns. Ajit the winner and Maya, the illusion. Illusion meaning that which appears but is not so. Like the idea of perfect love. Female virtue. Perfect life. Illusion meaning good luck because the illusion is the gateway to the truth. Once you learn of the name, it is possible to learn of the destiny. But there is one name that Suchitra loves but does not want to understand. She does not know that there will be many who will love the name Suchitra. *Su* plus *chitra.* She knows the meaning of her name but does not know then that for her, her name will become her destiny. To be a beautiful picture.

There is one name that Suchitra completely understands. It is the name of Ram. This one name, so unlike other gods who like to have many names. No, for this god only one name will do. A name destined to become synonymous with integrity.

Once there were three Rams. Ganga Ram, Sahib Ram and Ram Sharan. Grandfather, father, son. All of them except one was born to serve. Only one

of them could have chosen otherwise. A different
destiny. He could have been a Sahib. But he chooses
devotion. Like his favorite monkey god, the divine
monkey, Hanuman. Devoted to Ram. But Sahib Ram
is human; to be devoted to one means to be careless
with many others. His devotion will manifest itself
the day he and Suchitra hike to the Jakhoo temple
together. That day Suchitra will discover that Sahib
Ram looks at the world like her, that he is her twin
soul. The following day she will fall in love with JP.
She has only seen him once before from the height
of the box enclosure on the Ridge. Vantage vista
seats open to the exalted and the commoners alike.
She knows it the moment she sees the figure in a
newsboy cap that she wants this man who walks
like that. When this man in a cap comes home to
ask Daddyji for her hand, she will see the look on
Sahib Ram's face and realize that she is now on a
train when she was perfectly happy standing at the
platform. Suchitra wants to tell Sahib Ram, *I belong
to you, and so it is inevitable for you to lose me, to spend
the rest of your life dressing that wound,* but she says
nothing. She does not have the words. In time,
Suchitra will learn to make friends with words, find
the right words. But before she learns of the words,

she will build an understanding of names. What to call whom and why.

7

Ajit

She is asking me for mangoes. Just like I once asked her for cakes. She is asking for mangoes not for herself. Just like I once asked her for cakes not for myself. The moment she asked me, my mind was like, *yeah, but how, how mother, it's only early February and do you plan on sticking around till the summer?* The boardroom trains you into thinking about what cannot be done before you ask what can be done. Then when you are convinced that it cannot be done, you ask *why must it be done?* Why? Can you not sublimate the desire, mother, just like you made me sublimate mine once? But mother cannot sublimate, it cannot be done. Because to become an artist was my desire. To give the monkeys mangoes as a treat is her wish.

People often ask me what it was like to be my parents' son. One a painter and the other a photographer, both artists; one dead, the other close to dying. One never present in my life except in photographs, the other a large presence in my life.

My father, he was never present in my life. But I did see him once. Just a glimmer, the faintest hint, but I saw him even though we did not linger around long enough to talk. It was the year 1948. One evening mother came back from work early, dressed me in my best trousers and shirt and put a vest on me. "We are going to an exhibition," she had said. There are so many important looking people, no one bothers with us. He was dressed casually: kurta, vest and jodhpurs. His paintings stand out on the walls and he stands out in a group. She looks intently at each painting and every once in a while, she glances in his direction. He is always surrounded by people. He does not know that he is being watched. One minute I am looking at the colours on a painting, another minute we are running. There is someone after us. He is holding a few papers in his hand, papers he will throw away during the chase. It was JP. Mother grabbed my hand and said, "Don't stop running till I ask you to stop." And so we ran. My legs sting, my feet burn in their new shoes but I say nothing. After all, I am the man in her life now, I must be brave. We run from beyond Teen Murti to what is now the Rose Garden. I think he could have caught up with us, but he was not the kind of guy to chase after anything that wanted to run away from him. I have a feeling he must have cried that night.

How did we get to Delhi from Shimla? My grandfather, our Daddyji, is dead. India has just become independent. But mother only just wants to be. We take the steam train, now almost the toy-train. It's a long journey. There is no one waiting for us in New Delhi. But we have a place to go to, a job for her. The nuns have a soft spot for mother. When a woman who does not need a job asks for one, she must be helped. We are not refugees but we live like them, barely making the rent. Mother does not use her inheritance. How do I know that at the age of seven? I just do. We lose ourselves in the flood of people in Delhi. No one asks my mother, *"Where is this boy's father?"* No one knows where anyone is. The only way a country preserves its daughters' honour is by accepting everything and questioning nothing. Our landlord's wife and daughters adopt us; feed me when mother is busy writing stories and taking pictures. The only cooking she does is the *khichri* that she makes for me every day. Everything else comes from the landlord's family and our locality.

Still, it was a decent life. Mother did not get angry. She didn't offer too much attention. Just asked, "How is my Jeetu doing?" every now and then. The question not really a question. If I could change anything from that time, it would not be our *poverty*, it would be her crying. She cried. So much. Every night. *For the two of us,* she'd say. I thought of her crying as something that she had to keep doing, something as normal as an everyday act. Like walking. Like washing for hygiene. Like brushing for teeth.

Would things have been different if she would have waited in that apartment a few days more in London? Would JP have come back? Mother called my father once, a collect call. I don't know exactly how long after that night we ran from him we got that call, possibly a few months.

It's getting very, very hard JP. I don't know how... I don't know how...how...

The urgency with which mother uttered the word how reverberates in my mind all week. Then she put the receiver down and we walk back to our noisy neighborhood, to our one-room home. Mother washes her face and is done with crying for the day. She seems to have forgotten what she said to JP. What happened after that is unforgettable for both mother and I.

Four days later there is a knock on our door. We are startled. It's not late. No one ever knocks at our door at this hour. Mother is scared. Is Delhi rioting? Another knock. Finally, we hear someone speak. *My friend JP has asked me to visit Suchitra.* He keeps knocking. Mother does not open the door. Another man would not have returned. This time mother lets him in. He does not need much prodding. He works for the newspaper, India Times. He'd met JP in Goa, then again in Delhi. He looks like a newspaper man. Kurtas, yes, but not loose like those of politicians; his kurta is worn over fitted trousers, not churidars or loose drawstring cotton pyjamas.

Mother will only ask him his name. Swayam. Swayam is his name, this man whom JP has requested to visit mother.

Mother does not comment on the beauty of Swayam's name. He keeps sitting, although he will stop drinking the tea set in front of him. He will return mother's stare. On the day I marry Geeta, Mr Swayam will tell me that it was in that moment when he knew why he had been sent to Suchitra, why JP had begged him to visit us.

We fall into a routine. Swayam visits us every Friday. Takes me to the bazaar. He is always careful not to indulge me by buying too many toys or books. Sometimes he helps mother with the grocery. I can see then, even at my young age, that he looks forward to playing with me. Mother cooks more. Simple, innovative meals. Swayam and mother do not exchange many words. When they do, I see that they are very formal with each other. I am the focus of both their attention. Mother worries that I am maturing rapidly. If ever there is a moment when she seems to lighten up, her mood changes mid-sentence almost as if an amnesiac were restored memory. And with memories is what our sorrows are often tied with.

It's been almost two months since we've known him. An intelligent man never depends too much on human compassion; it's like election time goodwill the masses bestow upon the politicians. Mother is making tea by our stove. "I have a new job in Paris to collect and disseminate news. Ajit, would you like to travel with me to new places?"

Mother starts crying. Swayam keeps talking to me. All the other adults in my life so far have always abandoned me when my mother starts crying. But Swayam sticks with me.

They start making plans soon after. "We must consult with JP before we make further plans," says Swayam. My father, my father saved them the trouble. It was father's 29th birthday.

We sail again. This time in an aeroplane. Sahib Ram comes to say goodbye. I am happy to see Sahib Ram and happier to leave Delhi.

Mother is soon with child. When Maya arrives, I see her crying different types of tears for the first time. Sometimes I am jealous and I look at her intently while she kicks her socks off. Swayam always ruffles my hair at least two times on such days and reads to me every night.

Mother takes on a new lover and we all watch in amusement; it's her camera! Mother's camera makes her slim. She squats and lunges in our living room. We do not have much money but we always seem to have money for camera equipment. Mr Swayam never complains when mother spends on camera, lenses or films. He doesn't complain about her converting a room into a dark room to process films while we jostle for space in the adjoining room.

We move homes often and to the point that we know no one except each other. But we long to know someone else. Only mother gets her wish, every now and then. She's gone for weeks on end as we settle into a quiet life with Mr Swayam and each other.

After an assignment, when mother returns, she is angry and despondent. Things don't seem to go as planned for her. "Why is it so difficult? Is it because I am…" She complains, and he consoles her with a, "No, it is difficult work, Suchitra, you must be patient."

Mother does not like Swayam's explanation. She locks herself up in her room. He knocks. I can hear them arguing. Mother and Swayam argue for a while. Over time Maya and I have learnt to block them out. I am better at it than Maya. Gradually, Mother and Swayam settle into a routine, supporting each other and yet keeping room for disagreements.

Mother tells me when I am in high school, that she has been watching and she thinks that I should stop sketching; I do not have JP's talent. And it was so hard even with JP's talent. I want to tell her maybe it is harder when you have talent.

"You do not have your father's talent," she says, "not in the same measure."

"I know," I tell her that.

"Then why go down that road of suffering?" she says.

I want to tell her, beg her, to not take this away from me. This is the one place I get to be close to him. But mother reasons, cajoles, reasons strongly. Mother, of course, wins. I must, she says, learn to distinguish desire from destiny. She starts thinking. Economics. Then, a little later, business. Business? I want to be part of no one's business except mine. I want to earn nothing. Then one day I spot Geeta tying a bandana around her hair in the pool and I want all the money in the world. The day I start business school, I bring Geeta home. Mother was baking that evening. Swayam is away on travel. Mother is very polite and attentive towards Geeta and nods approvingly once I return home after escorting Geeta back to hers later in the evening.

Mother said to me once that it is inevitable to witness loss and death. I know, of course. Mr Swayam knew where the shoulder on the road was. A minivan parked on the shoulder. Unmoving. Mr Swayam got close, too close to stop, close enough to see that one of its windows had 'Wash me' written on its own film of dust. He skidded into the stationary vehicle. Mr Swayam had been wheeled away to the hospital by the time I got to the scene.

Mother's hands smelt of onion and saffron when I told her. She had been cooking. They were to have a party the following day. I walked inside; didn't know how to tell her. She started wailing immediately. She's gotten weaker since then. Like the opposite of a growth spurt.

Nothing is the same without Swayam, the man I avoided calling *Dad*. Only the sound of his footsteps is missing when I open the garage of the home in Bay Hills.

Swayam 'Swayam', the man who completed a half-written sentence, never afraid to work for happiness, to walk the long, long corridor to get to mother's heart. It's because of Swayam that we, we who were not supposed to be happy, stole so much happiness.

✳ ✳ ✳

8

First Times

It is early 1941. India is close to freedom. Suchitra will soon get some rest. She owes her return to Carmen Hall to a single line telegram that she sends to Bui. She will say, *Ajit cried without reason for the first time today.* Everyone at Carmen Hall knows who Ajit is; Suchitra has been writing letters to Bui. Daddyji will receive the telegram, give it to Bui after reading it. Sahib Ram will volunteer but Bui will gently brush off his offer. She will herself walk to the post office. Bui runs when she sees the postmaster locking the gates. She pleads with him to open the gates. The postmaster tells her he must lunch first and Aradhana will give him the look that will silence him, just like that look silenced her brother a decade and half ago when he asked her for her responses to the proposals of two young men he thought suitable for her. Bui doesn't have time to fill out anything; she will dictate and run back home. Bui needs to prepare the home for Ajit. Suchitra will sail the moment she receives the telegram. *All is forgotten. Stop. Come back. Stop. Love, Bui. Stop. Stop. Stop. A mother knows the condition of your heart from the faintest of footfalls.*

Now that she is back, Suchitra looks at everything through the prism of John Papi. Daddyji avoids Suchitra. Suchitra avoids Daddyji. Only Ajit seeks both of them out. And both Suchitra and Daddyji can't help doing the same.

Suchitra's mind wanders. The slightest tremor can take her to London, take her back to where she was writing letters. On that desk. The only thing that she feels belongs to her in these makeshift digs. Everything else, including herself, belongs to JP.

Suchitra will write letters; feed them week after week into the open mouth of a red letterbox. Even on the days when it is raining, she must feed her favorite red pet. Week after week word information, images, poems make their way to Bui. Not to Daddyji. These very airmail envelopes will announce to Carmen Hall the arrival of Ajit. Through a missed period, shyly at first. I am late, Bui. But Bui does not get that letter, does not acknowledge this *lateness* in her return letter. The urgency of it rises in Suchitra. She will say, *I can feel him.* There is no doubt in her mind that it is a him. *I can feel him fluttering in my tummy, like a butterfly.* Bui is ecstatic. Then sorrowful. This is not how it was meant to be; but this is how it is. Ajit will arrive. Crying. Wrapped in blood. Suchitra will make JP send Carmen Hall a telegram. It will be from Mrs Suchitra Matthews. Suchitra looks at Ajit and cannot believe it. She and JP made him together? All the time now Suchitra's gaze will be on Ajit. Taking for granted the one thing which she should not have.

As with all things in life, there were signs. From very early on. Seven weeks after they set foot on land, Suchitra showed up one evening unannounced at The Swatters Club while JP was having drinks with his group *(Surprise!)* and everyone was surprised. Even JP. Everyone looked at this girl with the same, obvious question in their eyes: *Who are you, walking inside this room with such ownership?*

She's my cousin, JP says hugging Suchitra close. Suchitra stares at him, still in his half embrace. JP begs for forgiveness later in the evening. Suchitra can feel her belly growing inside her. In a few weeks it will unmistakable.

Suchitra opens her eyes. It is morning. Not a foggy morning in London. A foggy morning in Shimla. Her belly has retracted. It is flat. Beside her sleeps someone who once lived inside her. Today he is four. Suchitra is no longer as careless with her appearance. No longer does she look through magazines with an aimless fervor. No longer does she jump from her seat at the mention of the words *art, painting, cap, heart, London.* It's a long list. It was Bui who knocked her out of it. It only took one sentence, "Stop, Suchitra, he will not return to us!" and Suchitra will never pick up *Life* again while she is in Shimla.

Suchitra and Daddyji talk to each other now. In so many ways, Suchitra is more educated now. In both formal and informal ways, Daddyji invites many suitors for Suchitra, both *one of us and not one of us* alike. Suchitra, in turn, quotes Daddyji to Daddyji, "Love is a dangerous luxury one must safeguard against."

Daddyji doesn't worry about the lack of a divorce, but he worries that he has another Bui on his hands. Another Aradhana. Someone who has no one to worship and whom no one will worship.

Daddyji is wrong on both counts about Aradhana, but right in his worrying about Suchitra. Ask Sahib Ram; Sahib Ram worries all the time. Quietly. Sahib Ram, he's a quiet one with dark circles under his eyes.

One evening Daddyji will ask Suchitra to join him in a celebratory dinner at the Clark. Bui offers to watch Ajit. Suchitra hesitates. But Daddyji, knows some things about Suchitra, he says, "No need to hide your face; it was our town before it became his." This sentence changes Suchitra's mind; she will join Daddyji for dinner.

After several years Suchitra is getting dressed for dinner. She wears a full-sleeved blue silk blouse with lace ruffles around the neck and a saffron and red sari with lace and golden thread zari work on the border. Bui is very pleased with how Suchitra looks. Daddyji smiles when he sees his daughter and asks Bui to loan her *some what are the things you women wear in your neck that stick to it?* as he put it. Bui will retrieve Sarojini's gemstone-studded pearl choker for her, but Suchitra will refuse; she is feeling suffocated enough.

On the way out, Suchitra bumps into Sahib
Ram and Ajit returning from their evening walk. Ajit
is in Sahib Ram's arms. Sahib Ram glances briefly
at Suchitra and then reluctantly looks away almost
immediately.

Suchitra asks him finally. "Why aren't you
happy now that I am back, Sahib Ram?"

Sahib Ram does not pause. The answer, it
needs no retrieval. It's there in the depths of his
consciousness, but also at the tip of his tongue.
"Because you are not happy, Babyji," he says as
he enters the glass doors to take Ajit inside while
Daddyji and Bui look on, teacups in hand.

It's a nice evening, despite the cold. They walk
for a while. When they near St Michael's Cathedral,
Suchitra feels very desolate, a lot more than usual.
Daddyji's words, *I am saying no because he's not one
of us.*

Because, because, because. For Suchitra,
nothing gets better even if the because shows up.
Daddyji walks a few steps ahead of Suchitra with

one of his new friends; today it is a young doctor. When Suchitra will tell Swayam about this doctor years later, she will be shocked that she remembers the details of the make of his cummerbund better than the contours of his face. Suchitra touches her face lightly. She is the Max factor lady tonight and it becomes her. This is the *good goop* Bui had introduced her the night JP came calling on Daddyji. The night she actually danced all night. The panstick cover suits her fine. As does the red lipstick that JP likes so much. Only the hair pins, so many of these pins in her hair, give Suchitra a headache.

It's dinnertime and Suchitra is introduced to many new colleagues of Daddyji. A difficult feat this in the snug hill town where Suchitra has been hibernating for a long time. She cannot help but think of all her first times with JP. The first time when Suchitra saw him—from the top of the highest point on the Ridge, her two best friends, Sarita and Padma, cackling behind her. A vantage point look at her life. The first time she met JP, Suchitra had something stuck in her front two teeth but JP betrayed nothing and continued intently with the conversation. Girls from Carmen hall would not have missed an opportunity to tease her. Bui might have discreetly pointed it out and asked her to 'tidy up'. Back at home, when Suchitra will look at herself in the mirror, she will feel a hot shame she has never felt before. Suchitra remembers the first time she wore her mother's white sari with a red border. But those days are long gone.

Bui can live because she remembers that Daddyji's refusal was well-intentioned. What, Suchitra often asks herself, must she remember to live so that she does not feel a stab of pain each time she looks at Ajit's face. Suchitra remembers JP throwing colour carelessly on canvasses and she wants to have a place where she can play too. The dinner this past weekend and Daddyji's growing kindness is unsettling her.

Suchitra takes more walks than usual. She often sits by herself on their bench. Nanga Baba is around this season. Suchitra has rarely heard Nanga Baba speak to any woman or pay attention to the musings of passersby. The cold does affect this ascetic. Sometimes the Nanga Baba flinches, but at other times he sits gazing vacantly at the cards in front of him. The only time Suchitra has seen the ascetic animated is when he is talking to his parrot. The only time he volunteers non-essential information is when someone asks him about his parrot. This parrot is one of a pair. A pair of lovers. Then no longer a pair when the mada died.

"Now, this old boy," laughs Nanga Baba pointing at his avian companion, "...is like me."

The childless couple who are the ascetic's audience this evening, smile, the man more heartily than the woman. Their omnipresent pain has been temporarily punctured, not by the humour in Nanga Baba's words but by his unexpected change in demeanour. The couple look light and cheerful, a remarkable turnaround in their spirits.

Suchitra, watching this exchange from twenty-five feet away, feels like someone switched on a fan in the room which holds her heart. There is air and it is not so oppressive anymore. A few days like this every quarter and Suchitra is hopeful that she can swim through life. Yes, only a few such moments, such days, are needed for Suchitra's heart to heal. This lightness persists even after the couple has left.

Nanga Baba is getting ready to leave for the day. The sun has set, bathing the trees and little mountainous hill ranges in an orange-reddish hue.

Suchitra gets up with an urgency that she does not know she still possesses. Seeing her run towards him, Nanga Baba stops folding his cards, lays them out again. This girl, he is happy that he has broken her reserve. The ascetic knows her name but does not display any sign of that knowledge.

Nanga Baba gives Suchitra two cards. The parrot has picked two cards. Two cards for one question. Two answers for one question. Two possibilities with the same last line on each card. Suchitra nods and smiles, then nods her head again, folding her palms together in thanks to the ascetic. It is possible, she wonders, that he—Nanga Baba—has been sitting with these placebo cards, shivering in the cold, just to give momentary solace to people like her.

Suchitra walks back fast, faster. She will be late for Ajit's dinner. She is embarrassed today by how she has slowly abdicated her son's responsibility to Bui and Sahib Ram. She knows this feeling; this intention will be short lived. But she can't wait to see Ajit. Ajit, ever ready with his smiles. Ajit, whose names means someone who cannot be defeated. Ajit, whose father abandoned Ajit and his mother Suchitra soon after his birth. Suchitra cannot help but marvel at the irony of Ajit's name. Suchitra walks faster; she is only about fifty paces, fifty steps away from Carmen Hall.

Daddyji and Suchitra are friends now; the animosity of the night when JP was refused forgotten. He cheers Suchitra up whenever she is feeling under the weather nowadays. "See, Suchitra, we are well. What did we have? Nothing. And now we have Ajit." Suchitra blushes and reminds herself that such thoughts are not welcome. She is angry at herself that Daddyji can still read her thoughts. Suchitra nods but thinks, *No, Daddyji, now I have Ajit and a broken heart.*

Daddyji, Bui and Sahib Ram have pieced together Suchitra's heart. Her heart has been pieced together but it is still aching. When she returns home that evening, Daddyji will kiss Suchitra on the forehead — the first day it starts snowing. Today it is not Christmas day, but two days sooner.

When she was leaving Carmen Hall, Suchitra said to Sahib Ram, "I don't want you to live alone." But he had already decided to live alone. There are days when Suchitra wonders if JP was there at all or if he was simply a figment of her imagination. Then she looks at Ajit and remembers, no, her imagination is false. Suchitra is true, *real.* She wonders if what Nanga Baba said to her will come true someday— that everything false in her life will have the opportunity to become true.

9

Waiting

It is February 2000. Ajit looks out of his window. A thin film of mist covers every window and only the few windows that get enough sun will become mist-free, unfoggy and clear during the day. The other windows will remain cloudy muddy, and Meena is too busy with things to even feel apologetic about not wiping the mist off the windows. Perhaps, Meena thinks to herself, *perhaps I will have some time to scrub the windows during the summer.* But summer is a long time away and Meena does not know what this summer will hold for her and Ram Sharan now that Suchitra is a member of their household.

Word has spread around Carmen Hall that Ajit's mother, Suchitra is home. One by one, the town trickles in. Ajit is surprised at how many of his mother's visitors are young people. Over and over they speak of the same story—*We heard of you from our grandmother, granduncle, from the exhibit in Delhi, from the speech you gave at the commencement...*

But really, they all are calling at Carmen Hall because of Suchitra's Bui and Suchitra's Daddyji and because Suchitra has remembered to return to Carmen Hall.

Others are there just because Suchitra is there. They do not know how and where they first heard of her. Some of them are Ajit's old playmates. Girls he played with as a toddler are women with grandchildren of their own now. Ajit's childhood playmates giggle and blush when he offers them tea and biscuits, the passage of time momentarily erased.

❅

Ajit sits on the chair in the corner, nodding to everyone. It does not help that it is a smallish chair, the smallest in the room. Occasionally he stands to greet and to escort someone to the main gates. Ajit is thick around the waist, but well-proportioned otherwise. Agile like a lion with deer reflexes. Stress sits uncomfortably on his forehead.

Ajit wants to start over, to rewind to that exact moment of genesis of his devotion to his mother. He wants to find his way to that moment and change its physiology, to be free from acceding to every request of his mother. Every except one unspoken one, and in that his marrying Geeta and by letting him do that, she had further deepened his allegiance to her by not asking him to.

The only respite in this relentless terrain of being his mother's son was Swayam. And now that Mr Swayam was gone, whom was he going to turn to? How was Ajit going to get mangoes for monkeys in February? Meena brought him chai, a cup of tea, a temporary reprieve from his own thoughts.

Meena always had a pot on; there were always takers for tea.

There was such a comfort for all at Carmen Hall in watching Meena do the everyday things — put cups and plates away in the wide-bottomed kitchen tray, draw the curtains, pull them apart, fold the blankets. And all this time, Meena's nose ring shone, a medium-sized gold hoop with a red jewel encrusted in its centre, akin to a lighthouse light viewed from the boat making its way from ocean to the shore.

✳ ✳ ✳

10

Ram Sharan

I am Sahib Ram's son. There begins and ends the story of my life. What does it feel like to be the son of a man who does not want your presence? Who did not feel the need to celebrate or express gratitude at your birth? I was his duty. Something for Maiye to live on, something that would take her attention away from having a husband only in name. I'll tell you what it feels like. It feels like nothing. To have and have not. Worse than not having.

Such a big saala fuss about dying. Dying like this and dying like that. Haan ji, when you live, you live like rajas and when you die, you die a certain way too. Aur kya? Haan, aur ab yeh bandar. Mangoes they will eat. Yes sir, raja ke bandar hai. They will eat mangoes for sure.

Before I met her, *she,* Madam Suchitra ji, was just a picture in my life. The most important photograph. I have seen Baba clean that picture on the mantel ever since I was a little boy. Seasons changed and that picture did too. The silver turned black. "That can be easily fixed." And Baba fixed the photograph.

Each year, I would discover later, just a week before her birthday, he peels the picture from the white sheet that supports it and away from the cardboard. The photograph was changing colour slowly. For that picture Baba had devotion, tenderness. And then that sandook. What valuables he guards inside that sandook! Then, one day when he was away at the doctor's with Maiye, I was 14, I pried open his sandook and saw, kuch nahin tha, just random things, things which belonged to her. How he beat me when he found out. One finger of mine still moves limp and slow because of that beating.

A few weeks ago he told me, "The lady in the picture is coming to Shimla."

Meena whispered to me, "She is coming to die in her childhood home."

I thought, Chalo aaacha hai, let's see what she is like now that the picture lady is coming to her home. Her home that has been ours for so long but never really ours because her invisible presence contaminates each room. I've hardly lived here; there's much to be done around the house and the city beckons me each morning. Baba, he lives in the room in the corner at Carmen Hall.

This father of mine has all his tenderness and devotion restricted to that photograph. Mother and I, we get cold stares, beatings, bottles smashed in that room which holds my books, books I am trying to use as a bridge to walk to another world. He cleans her home, runs it like a hotel, keeps her money safe, save for his income. He is only alert when he is doing Suchitra's work, other times he stares vacantly at anyone who will cross his path. Those very same vacant stares will slowly consume mother. Everything is duty for Baba. But what about love? The vermillion in her graying hair was once optimism, then duty, then resignation. All symbols. Nothing is real in our lives. Everything a symbol.

Everything is small in our lives, our sorrow, hidden and small. Only our names are large, king-sized. The rich, the privileged decide everything about their lives, even death. Saala die like this, and die like that!

I thought I escaped Baba when the collector said he would try to help me become a cook. Yes, life was better with the collector Sahib. So many years I trailed him, first as a temporary cook and then as the permanent one. But saali, there is good luck and then there is my luck.

We have one son. Only one child, I had said to Meena and she said *hai, why?* No one in her family is an only child. Meena asked me to reconsider, but I said nahin, atal nahi.

Why? Meena had asked. Because I will pour my everything in him. Better one diamond than ten false stones. And for once, god was kind. It was a boy. If it were a girl, we would have worked harder. But such a cruel society. You nourish a plant and then someone else takes away its shade. Fine, theek hai, but no one even says a thank you.

My boy, he went to Sanawar. Can you imagine, the son of a cook going to Sanawar? And such a wonderful boy he is, never ashamed of his Baba. Such a delight he is to everyone. The favorite of his teachers and collector Sahib. He became the head boy, then missed the civil services by a whisker.

But no mind; my boy is a Professor now in Dilli in a big college and what I said to Meena has come true. We poured all our water in his glass and he is not thirsty. And my thirst is not quenched but the pain has evaporated. My son, he is the peace I never had. Meena, my wife, such a good mother. Our son, he is her kindness.

Baba called me when she called him. *Baccha, I need help,* he said. And my wife, soft-hearted woman that she is, said, *chalo, chalo ji, he is an old man and we must go help him.* Kaun sa baccha? Kiska baccha? To have such a father is a punishment no one can be told about. But what to do, saali this duty thing is immiscible from our hindustani blood. So we, me and Meena, never anyone's personal servants, now serve *her*. To live in this house with her makes my mind hell, but what else is there to do?

Nowadays, he puts his hand on my shoulder, even asks me to wire money to his grandson. For Holi. *Holi blessings.* Yes, Holi blessings from the man who has wrung the colours from our lives to the grandson who does not need his money. He asks me how my shoulder is.

"Can you not see," Meena says to me at night, the night before she arrived, "he is asking for your forgiveness. Forgive him." *Forgive him?* How to forgive? Mere haat main hai kya forgiveness? I don't want his money and neither does my boy. Aur phir...what can an impoverished man give? Not even a bus ticket to sanity. Not a smile when you need it. What of Sahib Ram ji's useless money?

Forgiveness? But first I must understand him. And in order to understand him, I must serve her. Haan theek hai, she is something. But who burns his own house for a mirage? This Meena, foolish woman, taken in by their clear skins and useless polish, their soft voices; such naatak, I tell you. Naatak that the rich do to fool the poor. And what kind of rich are these people? Suchitra madam, her father was an army man, a servant of the people. Who knows what he was like? Yes, I have heard stories about his kindness. Then why did his daughter have to run away and marry? Why then did his beautiful sister die a spinster?

When *she* met me for the first time at Kalka station, she said, "So you are Sahib Ram's son. Come now..." and put both her hands on my head.

The touch of her half-cold, trembling fingers on my forehead felt nice. But then that feeling went away when I remembered who she was and more importantly, whose son I am. The son of a careless man. A duplicitous man; a man who behaves one way under her roof and another way under my roof. But under every kind of roof I am his son and how I feel suffocated under this weight of his name and Suchitra ji's home.

After we greeted Suchitra ji, we drove her home. It was a difficult ride for her. She doesn't speak much. The cold, the dip in oxygen is not good for lungs. I felt sorry for her then par us mein himmat to hai. Perhaps it is this courage that attracts Baba to her, for he has none, the spineless man that he is— beating a woman to prove his manliness, vacantly staring at the sun, throwing a plate full of food at an innocent woman for putting more salt in his dal, beating the son when he comes forward to protect his mother. Day after day, year after year, when the sun rises I see Baba looking at Suchitra ji's photograph with wistfulness, when it sets I see the rage in his eyes at another day gone by without setting them on his Babyji. Another day wasted because he had to make do with her pictures. A likeness, not the real thing. Such rage, rage. And we, Maiye and me, the receptacles for his vomit.

So I drove her home. Slowly. Something seemed to lift in her as we started unloading. Baba and Meena were standing outside near the large, iron gates and the gnarled pine. He smiles. She smiles. He doesn't move or come forward to greet her. It is us who take her towards him, me and the nurse, Rekha, almost like we are bringing his bride to him. Such nataak!

They speak in a formal Hindi but the intimacy is unmistakable.

"You're so late, Babyji. I thought a cloud burst on the way, Babyji, and you died under it..." he smiles, then laughs at his dark humor.

"Arre, Sahib Ram," she says and then pauses. It's cold, cold in bitter sort of way and I can tell that even this mountain girl is having trouble with it. "So many clouds have burst in my way, and I, I am so hardy, I still don't die."

"Like a cockroach, Babyji?"

"You remember well, Sahib Ram. Yes, just like

a cockroach."

Then they become quiet; their silence is comfortable, like nothing more needs to be said. Everything understood before it is said. That is how the silence of parents should be. Par hame kya pata? I never got to experience such parents.

Baba hovers around the rooms, not around her. Suchitra ji likes to be left alone. He watches everyone and everything that goes inside her room. Baba seems to know when she needs him. They speak briefly. I can overhear from the drawing room.

"I feel like I have forgotten Daddyji's face, Sahib Ram."

"No, Babyji, that is like forgetting your own face. I remember all of them."

Does Baba remember his wife's face? Does he remember the unspoken torment in her eyes? How can he speak, utter these lies so gently to this woman?

Then this gora boy arrives. A tamasha, a first rate one, if it was ever assembled. Then her son. He looks like a tall, middle-aged pehalwan. He struts about like a man comfortable with people doing his bidding. Always over-watchful. Smelling, tasting the curry, before Meena feeds her. He will point to things and mix his awful Hindi and English and say, *yeh karo, woh karo,* and then I want to raise my right hand to him and say, *kutte, main tera naukar nahin hoon, ask your original naukar.* But that original servant he treats with such deference. And by the way, I can do without your bekaar ki awful Hindi. I know English. I am 10th pass, you see. But it is my fate to keep waiting for people to find out things about me.

Speaking of English, the other day I heard her tell the gora boy, "Make a list of everything you want to ask, to learn and I will stick around till I answer all your questions." On better days, my heart asks me, how can you dislike such a person? But how can I like this woman? This woman whose presence on earth has been the source of all my misery? But in the presence of this woman, my father becomes the father I wanted him to be. And because of this moment, you are forgiven, Sahib Ram ji. And how do I show that forgiveness? By trying to find your saala mangoes. By praying for them. There are many mistakes we make in life—some in ball point ink, some in washable ink, some in smudge-proof ball point ink.

The biggest amongst them is being born. Birth is a fruit that never ripens.

11

Secrets

There are many moments from Suchitra's life that Jon will not know about. Many things that his questioning, speaking, filming, clicking, snapping will not bring to him. They are secrets. Not secrets because they cannot be told; not because their telling might bring shame, sorrow and devastation. They are secrets simply because no one knows where to go looking for them. Suchitra, for she has been designed as such, knows the most about her own self.

There are so many things Jon will never know: that the first one to pass was Bui. Then Daddyji. It is early 1947. Bui was lost to a slow pneumonia. There was some time for Suchitra to say goodbye to Bui but that still didn't change the question that kept popping in Suchitra's head—*why pneumonia?* Bui keeps herself warm all the time. Did Bui seek pneumonia? Or did pneumonia seek Bui? Suchitra will never know. Perhaps Bui had a premonition. Suchitra only remembers the facts and then depending on her mood, she retrofits them in a neat theory.

It is the beginning of the year 1947. India will soon become an independent country. Yet the mood on Mall road is not particularly celebratory. So many in this small hill town are readying to leave for England and for the New World. And Carmen Hall, with everything that has happened to it in the past few years, never quite made up with the word *celebration*. But now, Daddyji, Suchitra, Sahib Ram and Bui have Ajit and something inside them is thawing. It is January 1947. Bui displays her saris for selection. "Pick the saris you would like to have, Suchitra!" Suchitra wonders what brings this sudden urge to clear, sort and reorganize in Bui. However, Suchitra does not refuse Bui's generous offer and selects six of her favorite saris, carefully sidestepping the ones that were strictly Bui's. But Bui gives Suchitra those three saris as well.

The camaraderie and friendship between Suchitra and Bui is unmistakable.

Then Bui shows Suchitra that sari she wore when they, she and the Captain, took that photograph together. It is not cream like it appears in the picture, but a light peach with sparkles on the shoulder drape, the pallu and the border. Bui takes out the photograph and looks at it, then keeps it on her dresser. Bui takes the photograph with her everywhere, keeps it beside her when she eats her meals, when she sits outside to take her tea in the veranda. The mountains, right now snow-capped in front of her, her permanent tea party friends. No longer does she hide this photograph from Daddyji, a photograph whose existence has never been a secret from Daddyji in the first place. The day Suchitra wears one of Bui's saris, Bui sits down and makes sure that each sari pleat is in order, perfectly aligned and when she is finished, she tells Suchitra, "Do not feel sorry for me, *gudiya*. I have enjoyed every privilege marriage gives to a woman," and Suchitra knows what she means when Ajit walks in, hand-in-hand with Sahib Ram, and Bui immediately stops arranging the pleats for Suchitra and takes Ajit's hand.

Bui starts keeping a diary where she scribbles and transcribes poems, sentences from magazines. After Bui is gone, Suchitra will look through this journal. There is one sentence that will stab Suchitra deep in the heart. *What can a woman want when every breath is mine?*

Four months after Bui, it's July 1947, and Daddyji is dead. Just like that. Sahib Ram goes inside his room with Daddyji's morning chai and find out that Daddyji has no use for chai anymore. Sahib Ram will light the funeral pyre for him. He will tell Suchitra that Ajit did it but Ajit...well, Ajit will cry at the final moment, overwhelmed by the people, the noise, the clutter of departure. People all around Carmen Hall will pour in to give condolences to Suchitra, Sahib Ram and Ajit. One of them will be JP's mother, her mother-in-law in name. Except for the first day, Suchitra will not meet anyone. Sahib Ram meets everyone. He even takes care of Ajit. Suchitra has not washed her hair for over two weeks now. Sahib Ram feeds Ajit, who spends most of his day drawing and gets upset at Sahib Ram when he pre-cleans the room for the sweeper man. Over and over Ajit points to his sheets and says to Sahib Ram, "Do not the mix." Sahib Ram folds his hands and pulls at his own ears in response.

"Then, what else?" asks Jon. What else does Suchitra remember? *What else do you remember, Suchitra?* Suchitra remembers waking up in the mornings in a Carmen Hall bereft of Daddyji and Bui, soaking in the emptiness, of missing the one person who should have been with her at this time. She can hear JP mocking her, *What Suchi, where is your Daddyji's doctor now?* Suchitra remembers walking from one room to another with JP's voice ringing in her ears. She remembers walking down the Mall Road and feeling everyone's eyes on her and she remembers turning up the collar of her coat. She's the girl who has lost everything. She can hear JP again, *Good goody gumdrops, chappies, chappies, what's the rush?*

Suchitra remembers wanting to erase herself. There is not much light in the bathroom but the knife does not need much to shine. It shines, not a polished silver like sparkle, but a blinding shine for a dizzy Suchitra. Ajit knows what she wants to do. He stands outside her bathroom, knocking at her door. It is a gentle patting sound but relentless in its frequency. Sahib Ram is out, away to the markets. Even the sound of the water will not drown out Ajit's prayerful monotone: *mother, mother, mother.* Two days later Suchitra falls on the Persian rug, black, yellow and red, that had taken seven months to arrive. She resembles the protractor that Sahib

Ram remembers from his final year from school; they had only begun to use it and he loved what one could do with the protractor, provided one was skillful. Suchitra wants to faint but there is a sliver of consciousness left in her still. This sliver that will not die even under neglect, under duress. Just a glimmer, a glimmer that will make her look up, take her eyes to the ceiling, to the mantel. Her camera; it's there on the mantel, no fire lit under it, waiting for her patiently. Grief has been a good exercise for her soul. Suchitra decides she could use some exercise for the body too.

Sahib Ram and Ajit wait for her by the side as she moves around, taking pictures. Suchitra takes photographs of the usual suspects and venues first— the Mall road from the height of the Ridge vantage point, the children riding the ponies, the groups of tourists shivering as their discussion about where to eat becomes drawn out. Places where they cannot find a clean bench to sit on, Sahib Ram dangles Ajit on his knees; Ajit has been a good boy. Sahib Ram wants to give him something to eat, but they didn't come well prepared. They didn't know it would take this long. Neither did Suchitra.

Suchitra moves fast despite her thick black coat. Her muffler is the same amarayllis red that she has worn since senior school, something she will switch to calling a scarf once she reaches America. She realizes as she shoots these pictures that she knows nothing about her camera, like she knows nothing about herself. She knows not what light will do to the film, what darkness can bring to light. She knows no camera words—the only exposure she knows about is the kind that gives you a chill.

That evening Sahib Ram wished that Suchitra should grow old and die with him in attendance. He wanted so much to take care of her. The following morning Suchitra got up and promised herself that no matter what happened in her life, she would never kill herself and that this thing called death would have to come looking for her. It is the 16th of August 1947. India is independent and now Suchitra is too.

Yes, there are innumerable things that Jon will not know about Suchitra. But there are several things that Suchitra will not be able to guess about Jon either.

* * *

12
Searching

It is the 4th week of February of the year 2000. Carmen Hall is buzzing, tensely tiptoeing towards release. The atmosphere feels akin to the stress that surrounds a woman in the final stages of labor, every minute dense and full of possibility. Possibly catastrophic, possibly euphoric, but while there is a precedent for every infant who is born in this world, for every infant who will live to survive and grow or only just live briefly, there is no precedent for the anxiety that surrounds those who live in Carmen Hall.

"We've looked everywhere. We've searched everywhere. We've asked everyone." In the specialty stores on the Mall Road, in the lower bazaars, through contacts in the government, through contacts in the plains. Over and over, Ram Sharan and Meena tell their story again and again to disbelieving faces.

A few of the specialty stores shopkeepers suggested that they try mango pulp. "Readily available through the year. Equally tasty." At that

Meena would simply shake her head and start to walk towards the next store. Ram Sharan would adjust his cap and roll his tongue over the teeth behind his pursed lips. He did not understand why his wife was shaking her head, why mango pulp would not work, why it was important to have an oblong piece of matter with a hard core, its skin torn off, and its pulp devoured in that messy, unsatisfying way. And, he reasoned with Meena, *sometimes the mangoes are not even sweet, that not being a problem when you choose mango pulp.*

All this while, Ajit has been standing on the sidelines, frozen and numb. When he noticed that Meena was often late, he decided to join her and Ram Sharan on their daily trudge. His Hindi had been out of commission for a long time, but Ajit was a quick learner. He watched Ram Sharan and Meena in action and then within three days he was accosting strangers, with no logical reason, except for his heart telling him. "Yes, ask this one, or that one," and he continued telling everyone the story of his mother and her wish for mangoes, spreading the seeds as far and wide as he could. Not ours to see when they sprout, if they sprout. As for Ram Sharan and Meena, their tape grew scratchy after a while.

Yet they soldiered on. Not with the same ferocity, but they kept on, until they had extinguished all possibilities. They then retreated into a corner, awaiting a miracle, or any other directions from Ajit.

Sahib Ram is at home—exchanging notes with the doctor on the telephone, watching Suchitra, watching the nurse, watching himself. He can see that his son is unused to this waiting, the patience it demands, how it feels like being dunked in ice and fire at the same time. They are waiting, Ram Sharan and Meena, for Ajit to unlock something.

Ajit does not know what to do. At night he spends long hours with Geeta on the phone, briefing her meticulously about the day. *The doctor says we must try to send her happy.* "Ajit, we don't need a doctor to tell us that!" Geeta snaps at him and despite themselves and their tension, they laugh. Geeta is upset she is not there, to understand the situation on the ground, to make decisions. But the boys need her to be where she is, and Maya does too. So they will delay her arrival till when it is absolutely urgent. Ajit and Geeta's despair is growing. They are used to solving problems together. But now it is becoming clear to them that this problem is not theirs to solve. This is between Suchitra and someone else up there. They are simply there to be a witness. To success. To failure. To be Suchitra's hands and legs. But Suchitra is still in possession of her mind and heart. Suchitra is still in charge of her own will, its depths and surfaces, grooves and ridges.

Ajit and Geeta feel destroyed. Let down. Like they've lost a race after having an unbeatable lead. After he's done talking to his wife, Ajit does something he hasn't done in a long, long time. He has most definitely not prayed since Swayam left the world. When Ajit slips into sleep, his hands are still knotted together and placed on his chest.

Jon has been kept away from the physical logistics of this search. Like a child, he has been only troubled by the existence of a problem, not with trying to find its solution. And just like a child, he is very troubled with it nonetheless.

Suchitra is groggy in the mornings after nights of fitful sleeping, so Jon keeps the mornings for himself. His room is nice, roomy and cozy at the same time—at the far end of the house—it has soft sheets, a lamp for reading, a TV and an empty cherry oak cupboard to put away his things. The first week he does different things every day, things a tourist would be expected to do: get photographed in the hilly costume, usually with a borrowed baby in lap as the surprised parents look on, learn to navigate the way from home to the Mall road independently, try the thanda, fresh apple juice and visit the Jakhoo temple, the institute of Advanced Studies. But it was the Mall Road that was to become his everyday staple. On this road, colorful thick sweaters, shawls and scarves abound as do the cameras slung around necks. Here, Jon, with his big, fat camera, does not stand out. But Jon, he does not know how to blend in. It is this immiscibility of his that has brought him court summons. Summons taken to their summit that had ensured that he would now see Jake by appointment only, kind of like seeing a dentist, just more frequently.

Carmen Hall and Suchitra kept Jon busy. But still not busy enough that he could keep his thoughts at bay. It was the routine of the mornings that Jon missed the most—the sizzle of skillet on Sundays. Then he remembered that it was better this way.

Jon found the monkeys just as fascinating as

Suchitra. He made himself unobtrusive and started filming. He started with still pictures. He was in love with the monkeys too, not in some exotic way but with the curiosity that a person has for someone almost like oneself. He filmed them relentlessly. The monkeys, on their part, avoided Jon. Made faces at him. Raised their fists at him. But he was undeterred.

Jon wore them out. Just like Suchitra and the rest of the household, the monkeys too had come to accept him. And perhaps even love him. And perhaps because on the days when Jon photographed them, the eagle seemed to leave them alone.

Now they posed for him. Like a woman who comes to dress for the bothersome, unwelcome admirer who follows her from the bus stop to her destination, day after day. Now they wear their photo faces for him. The monkeys are tireless. Just like Jon. Nightfall disbands their play. But it's merely a pause.

✳ ✳ ✳

13

Suchitra

Everything is always better in the mind. Stories. Colors. Dying. Only the intoxication of living, only that is better in life. Bit by bit, everything has been taken away from me. Then why build when everything is given only to be taken away? Mother, Daddyji, Bui, JP, my boy with Swayam, Swayam, this vitality. The only thing I have now is my josh. My enthusiasm, my will. In the end, we come back to the beginning. We ask ourselves: Was it satisfactory? Was it worth the time? The humiliation? One memory folding itself into another.

The boy, Jon, asks me which was my first camera. The first camera? It was the camera our landlord in London, Mr Peeko, gave me on the day I decided to sail back to India, two days after JP left me, Ajit and the apartment with nothing but two months' rent. They returned the rent money and gave me the camera when I told them that JP had abandoned us. When I am temporarily done with crying, Mr Peeko and his wife Sheri will come help me pack. London is expensive, and I must now sail back to where I came from. Now I have Ajit to look after as well.

Mr Peeko will drive us in the Rolls, the only inheritance that his wealthy father will leave him. Everything else will be washed away in the debts. "It eats everything but isn't it something?" Says Mr Peeko. Sheri and I will sit behind. I have lost JP. Now that I am leaving she will lose the opportunity to see a child grow in front of her.

We stand on the docks looking absently at each other for a long time. But Mr Peeko plays a game with us. "Tell me," he says, "my cherie, which country do you think I was born in?"

We have played this game many times before. He has pale skin, he has a tan. His accent, the schools have scrubbed him of any telltale sign. I lose over and over. Mr Peeko refuses to tell me. "You must find it out yourself."

"Tell me, Mr Peeko. I hope it is a country where people do not break each other's hearts." I don't care that everyone is looking at me.

"In every country you will find some people who will not break each other's heart," says Mr Peeko, half smiling. "Everything gets washed away in the waters. Let it wash away, everything. He will come back to you."

I say nothing.

On the ship, ready to board. Ajit is almost two. Mrs Peeko, Sheri, will tell them that the boy will be two soon. They bring out cakes. Sometimes people will even offer to hold him for me so that I can get some rest. I have been doomed to be restless, I will mostly refuse. Some days when I must, I cry. I will hand over Ajit to someone and let the salty humid breeze make my face wet. I wonder if I will ever sail again.

I want to fear being face to face with Daddyji. I want to fear their reaction to Ajit. But the only thing I fear is myself. How will I live with this person who says nothing to someone who informs her that he is leaving her? That and Daddyji's slap. It was Daddyji's slap which drove me into JP's arms. And then JP abandoned us. That is what the tale is.

Daddyji slapped me. And it was not for myself that I did not let his slap hold me back. It was for all the other people he kept slapping, slapping and no one ever did anything about it. He would no longer choose for all of us. Be it wrong, right, whatever, no more for all of us. It never occurred to me what would be the price of that slap. I began to have a sense of the price of that slap when JP lost himself deeper and deeper in that model who was supposed to take only her clothes off for him.

Life feels like a scratchy record when I return home. Nothing sounds like it once used to. I am no longer the old me. The new me is not yet formed, it doesn't want to be born. I had thought that the sight of the monkeys on the Ridge, in Sanjauli, in Jakhoo will enrage me. I am wrong. When I see the monkeys, I realize that they are the only place where there is no shadow, where I am not troubled by my present. Yet, I am not what I once was. I cannot give my monkeys their mangoes. I am full of blemishes.

After Daddyji's passing, I leave home. Because I have no one. Yes, I have Sahib Ram but not really. All these people Daddyji feed and honored? Where are they? Where did they disappear to now that my

Daddyji is gone? I have Sahib Ram, but as long as I live with him, he cannot start his story. And I have nothing to start over. I am simply waiting for the inexorable pull of the end. I speak to Sahib Ram more crossly than I have ever done before. I have to leave. But Carmen Hall never leaves me. My monkeys do not leave me. I remembered those monkeys all the time, even while waiting alone in the labor room halfway through sketching a beautiful body. Their red faces and baby hands beckoning me, the face of my child morphing into a simian likeness over and over. It's only after Maya arrived that the monkeys were pushed away.

It was the monkeys who pointed me to the biggest sparkle of my career. I have been writing, taking pictures for 15 years now. Work is not steady, only my intent is.

Intention. I think it is time to let go. I have neither Swayam's skills with facts, nor JP's love of colours. Now I enter this room. I have the keys. I keep clicking photograph after photograph. It is the intent. It feels like it will never be done. Our debts are mounting. No one gives me work anymore. I tell Swayam that this is my final hurrah. I must do something else, find some way to be useful, or we must return to India, where we have roof over our head unencumbered by mortgage.

"You must create a series of photographs," Swayam suggests. I don't know, I say, I am not ready. That night I dream of monkeys. I dream of Mr Peeko giving me the camera, with monkeys sitting beside me on the bench near Mall Road. Inspired by the dream I decide to make one last series of photographs. It is those photographs that brought me the honor in my career. I called those series of photographs, *Intention: the exhibit*. Photographs of people with intent, with an aim in life. The first camera is the eye. My eye. This eye that blinks. Cries. Sleeps. Opens. Rolls. Wakes. I put myself in Swayam's hands and he lets me fly. It is those photographs that brought Jon to the exhibit and then eventually to me.

This boy, he looks like my painter. Not in the likeness of face but his demeanor, his restlessness. He has brought upon himself what my painter brought upon himself. You cannot flee love. Because death is coming anyway. And if you flee love, then you have to flee yourself. Just like my painter.

My feet are getting cold; the cold travelling up the neck. The end of all stories is the same.

The first week Ajit came to Shimla, I asked him, "How long will you stay?"

"I'm just taking some time off," he answers, his eyes steady on the fanless, barren ceiling.

"I might not die as quickly…"

"Even better," he says quietly, kisses my right three fingertips which are placed on the pillow and then he is gone.

But it is all in the past. Now Meena plays songs on Vividh Bharti for me. Only Ajit and Sahib Ram are still in the frame. In the present. Ajit comes back as Meena is feeding me dinner, sabudana in milk with a hint of sugar and cardamom. I speak with difficulty. The pain killers make me groggy. Tomorrow, if I get a tomorrow, I am going to ask Ajit to reduce them in dosage. Meena holds a full spoon in front of me patiently, she brings it close, closer to my mouth. I can barely swallow. It's like being numb, the liquid spills down my lips. The jaw, upper jaw, swollen like a Hanuman mouth, the lower still mine. But I don't care, I am shameless. No bib, nothing. I let her feed me. Then fret when she insists she must sponge me now that I am wet.

"We've been trying, mother, it looks like it's going to be hard." I keep silent. "It's going to be hard, mother," Ajit repeats.

I say. I want to scream it, but it is too much effort. Sarcasm is just right. It never failed on his father and it doesn't fail on him. But the exertion, it makes me feel dizzy, faint. Where will I fall if I'm lying in a bed? How is it possible to feel like I am falling? I am already lying in a bed. But I feel like it anyway.

"Mother, mother!" Ajit brings me back.

"Mangoes," I tell him, *remind him*. "I will wait."

"Apples? Apples are sweet too." I hear a desperation in his voice, a desperation I longed to hear in his father's voice. It was not satisfying when I finally got to hear it. "We can have Meena mash them, even make something with them."

"Mangoes," I tell Ajit. "Apples are apples, mangoes are mangoes. It's only late February.

Apples are sweet too but we can wait." I say after waiting a long time. Such a long sentence. I am tired.

After February comes March. Cold March. Mangoes are many weeks away. I failed my monkeys once. Will I fail them again? It's all JP's fault. JP, when I meet you, I will not speak to you.

14
Photographs

The first ever photograph that Suchitra will see will be that of her mother. The photograph that will change Suchitra's life will be the one which Bui will show her of herself with the Captain. Bui is in pigtails and a sari that looks beige-cream in the picture. The Captain is looking straight at the camera, one hand in his pocket, the other around Bui's shoulders. He is wearing his tweeds. Bui is suppressing a smile and looking straight at the camera. But what Bui will not allow her lips to show, her eyes will do for her. Suchitra has a feeling that soon after this photograph was done with, the Captain might have looked at Bui for a long, long time. That feeling is validated when forty years later Suchitra will meet the Captain and he will look at her the way he might have once looked at her aunt. When Daddyji dies, Suchitra knows that the photograph is more than his likeness. Soon, the photograph will supersede actual moments and serve for an emotional shortcut, an energy supplement, almost like a vitamin for when the day's energy levels are lower. The photograph, it becomes Daddyji itself. To feel Swayam's presence, Suchitra needs no photograph. Of course, she has the maximum photographs of Swayam in her possession.

Swayam 'Swayam' feels heavy. He has overslept. He does not feel light even after bathing, breakfast or the walk to work. When he looks at the morning's printed wires, he realizes why he felt that way. It is just a simple, four-line news flash with a photograph that Swayam would read in the wires. Young India is still discovering JP. The long, glowing obituary will have to wait a few more days. Swayam is the first man in India besides the man who transcribed and set the wire to learn of the news. He wonders if he should hurry to Suchitra but decides against it. Suchitra will learn of it in the afternoon when she turns on the radio. As usual. But the news, it is no more the usual for Suchitra.

Swayam shows up at her doorstep soon after. He does not ask her how it feels. She keeps repeating the words *plane crash, plane crash, plane crash* like they are some kind of a mantra. Then when she's had her fill of those two words, she will choose another word. Why? Swayam will hug, kiss her for the first time in that moment. The kisses will do it. Suchitra will break down. She will close her eyes and inside her wet eyes, she will see a fallen newsboy cap on Mall Road. Even in her dreams and thoughts JP Matthews has abandoned her now. The only place he will be accessible now is in photographs. How many does Suchitra have of him? No one knows this about Suchitra and this will not change. But whatever that number, zero to infinity, JP has now been rendered unforgettable by his absence.

In most families in Shimla, it is the men who take photographs. Once they have pressed click, they feel that they have done their bit, their duty ends here. It is the women who then catalogue them. This is the division of labour—to men, the job of trying to forget and to women, the job of remembering. Suchitra has changed that.

Sahib Ram is twenty-seven, just a year older than Suchitra who is now in Delhi, the capital of partitioned and free India. He does not have too many photographs. The ones he does are the postcards sent by Suchitra every two weeks. On one of those postcards, Sahib Ram tells her that he is to be married, compliments of his father's forgotten first cousin settled in Hamirpur. His aunt tells him that she is very nice, almost as nice as Babyji.

The harsh climate makes people's hearts grow cold, covetous, drying out praise and adoration from their hearts.

So many photographs, boxes and boxes full of them. When she starts getting famous, it is a relief for her, for *them*; it is a relief when they can donate. Their junk is valuable to some people. A man who she had thought spoke the language of her heart, by that one action he made himself a stranger to her heart; this man who had the restraint of a man but none of the love that a man should have.

Jon has always been fascinated with photographs. When he has the camera in his hand he wants nothing else. From one army base to another

and then to—for what at that time felt like forever—
Gran's home, only the camera being Jon's constant.
It is the only thing that he has asked for in his life
and received at the right time, the only thing he
did not have to beg for, the only thing that was not
denied to him even though at all the other times he
has not always been undeserving. Then comes the
day he will walk through the doors of a museum.
He has met Suchitra before but never fallen in love
with her this far. He is in a familiar territory with
photographs on walls. He feels restored; feels as if
there is a resonance from his heart that is echoed by
each of those photographs. He feels clean, tidy, like
everything has been neatly filed away in drawers
in his head. But that feeling starts to evaporate the
moment he starts walking away from the museum.
It is clear to Jon. He must find more of this medicine
or else he will sink. He cannot drown. He is so heavy.

✳ ✳ ✳

15

Jon

I ask her boring questions. *What type was your first camera? Who gave it you? When did you learn to develop your own pictures? Did people wonder what a woman was doing with a camera?* She answers when she can. Other times she laughs. It is not the feeble laugh of a sick person; it is the full-throated laughter of life. There is nothing old about her. Everything is fresh. Suchitra likes it when I make assumptions about her.

I ask her, "How difficult?" Suchitra becomes silent and does not answer me for another day. But that was only one day. For the most part I stay silent. She stays in one position for a long time and maintains eye contact with me and when it becomes supremely uncomfortable, she turns. They didn't want me around. But now that I am here, I am another pair of eyes, another set of legs, hands. They like me to photograph. Her son, Ajit, has been preoccupied ever since she asked for the mangoes. Suchitra scared us today. Her breathing became labored, shallow, sporadic and heavy right after the doctor gave her an injection to help her sleep. She came around, but then we were worried that she'd slipped into a coma. When Suchitra awoke, there was a mini celebration, almost like a holiday party.

I like that India is noisy. I want to lose myself in the noise all around me, forget the voices inside my head. But Carmen Hall is where I am now and Carmen Hall is always quiet, even when people talk.

It was Maya who sent me to Shimla. I found out where Suchitra lived the moment I was done with the exhibit. I simply had to see her. But I reach her home and the nurse is directing the movers. I lie about my profession to Suchitra's nurse, tell her I am a journalist. She tells me about Maya. Maya can see through my lies. She is an edgier version of Suchitra. I try to charm her. It doesn't work. Then I cry. Without knowing why, I cry. And Maya writes down the address on a piece of realtor freebie paper and makes me promise that I will not share this information with anyone else. I have kept my promise that I will not tell anyone where Suchitra has gone to spend her last days.

I had no doubt in my mind when the plane

took off that Suchitra would approve. But a part of me was afraid before I saw her. Afraid, you know, of being disappointed. Like Nana used to say how the name of God is better than God himself. I read copiously on Suchitra.

Suchitra is not like the other old people I have met. It was clear from the get go: *What can you get from an old girl like me?* There are no rehearsed stories, no story told so many times that they are sharp like diamonds. The first few days she answered some questions. Then she grew very interested in me. She's smart. A few hints and she understands. She suggests I go here, I go there, visit places. Every day, it's a new place. *Go to the ridge. Go to the church.* Some days she asks me to take pictures. Some days she says no camera. *Just the eyes.* Some days she wants to hear how my day went. Some days she'll ask me questions: *Is that bench still there? How many people were on the streets? What were they wearing?* People are kinder to me when I tell them I am staying at Carmen Hall; everyone seems to know Suchitra ji.

When I return to Carmen Hall, I say nothing

most of the times. Suchitra is not perturbed by my silence. On days that I am so full that I want to empty myself in front of her, she will not ask but pretend to be so ill that even listening will hurt. But on the days when she will listen, a half hour is worth a lot.

Every once in a while she will ask me an unusual question—*What is waiting for you at home? What do you typically do when you want something?*

She knows that nothing is waiting for me at home. But she does not know that I met her on the day it became clear that nothing would be waiting for me at home, if ever I had a chance.

I kept walking from the court, kept walking, walking, just walking and doing nothing, nothing to reduce the tension. And then I grew tired, really tired, when I saw a long line of people outside the Asian Arts Museum. I just stopped. I could have kept walking, but I was hungry. I wanted to sit somewhere, some place warm. Somewhere, where there were people. People not in a rush to get somewhere. And the exhibit is how I found Suchitra.

✽

Then the nurse, I find her outside the home, the home that will never be sold.

"How do you spell your name?" Sahib Ram asked me. "If you alter the sounds just a little, it becomes josh, *enthusiasm.* Where is yours?"

She just keeps sending me places. Go somewhere. "Where?" I ask? Ask Sahib Ram, she says.

Sahib Ram sends me to Chail and Kufri to see the palace. The cricket ground.

Suchitra ji doesn't talk much about her husbands. The first one she calls her painter. The second one is just *him.* Always *he* said this, *he* said that. *He* did. *He* went. *He* is ever present.

Last night she said to me, "My painter could have been a cricketer."

I can picture her there in her school girl uniform. John Papi Matthews at the bat. She is looking at him. But she does not know that he is also looking at her.

I can see all this in front of me. "Tonight," I said to Suchitra, "I will tell you a story." And I told her this.

"How did you do it?" She asks. I say it was there in the air. I just needed a little help from a photograph. She beckons me to her bed, raises her hand and again know just what to do. My head and her fingers in my hair. For this touch I have travelled oceans, for this benediction with just a little help from a photograph and the story of a divine monkey.

Sahib Ram asks me, "Where is your josh, your enthusiasm, young man?" Where is my enthusiasm? I think I left it in the courthouse.

This Sahib Ram person, to say that he is *odd* is an understatement.

For everything now Ajit too suggests I ask Sahib Ram.

They are a motley group. But an odd family is better than none. And now I am family too. They are ill too but they have medicine. He has her. He is troubled by her. But he has her. He is always going to have her. Where is my medicine? Why did you send me in this world when no one wants me here? This is one question I cannot ask anyone, I cannot utter to anyone except in the bottom of my heart.

Yesterday she said to me, "Do whatever anyone asks you to do today." I did not understand what that meant at that moment. I do now. I have bought three sweaters in thick wool from the Tibetan market, danced with a group of Sikh turbaned men with beards, flirted with a group of college girls.

Now I am home. I am tired. I wait for Mrs Meena's cooking. Tomorrow I will wear one of my sweaters. They are nice, heavier than what I wear. I got them at a good price. She said to do whatever anyone asked of me. So when the most persistent vendor in the wool market needed my cash, I could not bring myself to refuse.

The good price was negotiated by two passersby's *"don't fleece the boy"*.

I am the outsider here but then, why do I feel like I am the only person she trusts? Trusts enough to tell her story, her true story to the world. "I knew of her, yes, long before," says Sahib Ram. Whenever the subject of Carmen Hall comes up, Suchitra calls Sahib Ram and they both talk about Carmen Hall. Sahib Ram hovers around us when we talk, trying to pretend that he understands something. That he is onto something.

"Just keep the good memories, they will help you along the way. Happiness is an intention. That's all. Keep the photographs," says Suchitra. "They will remind you that you have been loved."

Then there are the monkeys. They are crazy, so so crazy and there is this eagle that keeps spying on them. Almost like he is eying the little guy in their troop. She sighted them.

Then she asks me a question. "What do you do when you want something?" So many interviews, so many committees, no one has ever asked me a question like that.

"Either you go after something, that which has been forbidden. Or, you stop wanting it."

"But there is a third way," says Suchitra, "which is waiting to receive it."

They are not right about the eyes. I am many pairs of eyes. I see everything. *Click. Click. Click.* File. Save. Sometimes Print.

✳ ✳ ✳

16

Mango

It's 1940. Suchitra wakes up this August morning craving mangoes. This is not a craving Sheri can satisfy. She tells JP this over breakfast, half-expecting him to mock her, to tease her about the moment that brought them together, but he says nothing, only kisses her lightly on the forehead and leaves. Ajit is sleeping in their bedroom. No longer their bedroom. Now it primarily belongs to Ajit

What Suchitra does not know is that JP leaves their home each morning but he has nowhere to go. He walks the streets aimlessly, takes his sketch book with him everywhere, but he has not picked up a brush in three months. Suchitra has noticed that but assumes that he must be painting at school, in his master's studio, probably working so hard that he doesn't feel the need to bring it home.

JP is sitting on a bench. Not their bench. It is raining and he has forgotten to bring an umbrella. He usually walks but is sitting for a change. JP has been walking for two weeks now. Walking in the sun, in the rain, on cold days, on dark days, since the day he has decided that he can no longer be an apprentice. JP can no longer apologize for the colour of his skin.

✣

In their apartment, Suchitra is trying to paint. The colours are elusive. JP makes it look easy. Suchitra is about to give up in frustration when Ajit wakes from his nap, crying and calling for her. Suchitra is happy that she has a reason to abandon her painting.

JP has not only abandoned his teachers, but also all his models. If you ask him, he might say that it is the other way around. When he sees Suchitra pregnant and her symptoms start manifesting, he thinks, *this is exactly how I am, the only difference is that strangers are kinder to Suchitra and Suchitra will deliver, be free someday.*

JP thinks he knows just how much he loves Suchitra. And Ajit. His Ajit. He thinks of Daddyji a lot this year too—the one time when he and Suchitra's Daddyji were face to face, that time when Daddyji asked him if he has an offer for a job in London too, besides the offer to study, to learn.

Daddyji asks him over soup, "What about employment?"

"A job?" JP asks without looking up from his soup.

Daddyji nods. "A job like everyone has, something which involves getting up every day and going to the same place?" Daddyji is glaring at JP now. "Yes, something like that."

"Yes, I will get up and go to my studio every day."

On that bench, in the rain, with Suchitra and Ajit safe in their apartment from the rain, JP realizes that Daddyji was right. A mother and her child need a man who will take a job. A man who will allow a job to do to him what jobs do to men.

It's a long year. Suchitra now no longer cares about what is going on in the world. She only cares of her own heart. No more newspapers are read by her.

Ajit is sleeping. Suchitra feels such tenderness rise inside herself each time she puts him to bed. In that moment she does not feel that tinge of loss, recrimination, anger like a heady cocktail that she takes a swig from with each breath. No, when Ajit is being rocked to sleep, she is not the girl who has disobeyed her father, the wife who is hungering for her husband's undiluted attention, a young woman aching for her Bui. But the moment he is asleep, Suchitra wants to wake him up. Tell him things. Teach him things. Pour herself into him but keep his mould intact. Now that she has her Ajit, Suchitra is interested in the future. She makes a mental note to go seek Nanga Baba once she is in Shimla next. But when and how will the next time be? Suchitra's mind races to the first time she saw JP. The first time, the first time Suchitra saw JP was from the bell tower at the Ridge. It was a Sunday. Now, JP exchanges nothing with her. No words, no bitterness. Just silence. Lots of silence.

JP is wet, soaking, drenching wet. He is still on the bench. Not too many people have continued sitting on this bench even as it pours. This now makes it his bench. The newspaper which he had spread between his legs is wet too. The ink is smudged, the words slowly swimming into each other. He looks at a man and his young son as they hurried across the street to take shelter in a butcher shop. He remembers then that he is a father too now. He is wracked by worry for the first time. John Papi, who has never thought of the future now thinks of it. What will it be like? Will his son become like him? Nothing would displease him more.

On top of the list of things Suchitra wants to teach Ajit is something quite useless. It's the same thing she wanted to teach that sloppy baby monkey. Suchitra had been sitting on the bench, waiting for John Papi for over a quarter of an hour when she dozed off. It was the baby monkey whose touch woke her. Suchitra has eaten many mangoes this year. The season has been good. How to eat a mango? You will need a knife, fingers, teeth, tongue. But most of all, you need a heart that loves and a mind that knows when to remember and when to forget.

❉

That night JP looks at Suchitra's sleeping form and realizes how much he loves her. This flower that he thought could be his. But it was time to place it back in the bouquet.

17

Failing

It is February 2000 and Ajit has grown increasingly irritated at Sahib Ram and his son. Angry at Suchitra for making such an unreasonable demand. Mangoes for monkeys in this season, who would believe it? They have tried everything. He has now given up.

Suchitra keeps her eyes closed through much of the daytime. Ajit does not know if she is sleeping or unconscious or pretending to sleep. He can barely sleep at nights himself. He misses Geeta and the comfort of her body. He misses the comfort of her taut, dense bones on a still girlish body. He misses his boys. Misses the games that have been won or lost behind him. Most of all, he misses Swayam. The man he never called Dad.

He is grateful for Jon. Because he is a link to the world that Suchitra has left behind. When Jon is around, they think about, talk about other things. Jon symbolizes happier times to Ajit, moments when his mother was able-bodied. Aspirational. Angry. Achiever. They revisit the world of photographs a second time. The photograph, a shorthand for emotion long gone and not replaced. He wants that mother of his to come back for a few moments and bring herself the mangoes. Mangoes for Suchitra's monkeys.

No one believes that they will find the mangoes, no one except Meena. Therefore, besides Jon, Meena too has cultivated a friendship with the monkeys, albeit of a slightly different nature. Jon and Suchitra were so busy talking about photographic plates that they scarcely paid any attention that today the contents of Meena's *tokari* were different.

Ram Sharan was the only one who noticed. Today his wife was taking them some bananas. The monkeys had been offered apples a few days back. The apples were rejected. Bananas, on the other hand, always safe, always welcome. Only Meena in her motherliness seemed too eager for a change.

Everyone feels inexplicably buoyant when they see Meena return with an empty *tokari*, the basket to hold fruits. But as the evening comes upon them, this mood fades and unlike the sun, it will not return the following day, even if it be for a brief while.

The chai becomes cold even as Meena pours it in cups and takes it for the men. They lose electricity that evening. It does not return until the next afternoon. They keep Suchitra warm with the heat of a generator, some extra blankets and a gentle fire which burns in the adjoining room to avoid further irritating Suchitra's cough.

18

Ajit

Would life have been different if she would have stopped for him that night? Would he have lived? Would we be here in this moment, longing for mangoes?

Somewhere in between these crumpled sheets and heavy quilts, mother is there. And this will. Mother said to me once, "Except love and life, money can buy a lot of things." False reasoning that she used to build my life on. "Doesn't that count for something, darling?" No, mother, you were wrong and I was right, even though I am living your wrong. Money buys nothing. Make no mistake. Nothing. Not even your mangoes. I want to ask her to stay two more months and I will fill your room with mangoes to touch, to bless, all kinds of mangoes—alphonsos, langras, dusheris...

Yesterday she could turn both sides. Today the left side will no longer let her and she is frustrated. Somewhere in between these crumpled sheets and heavy quilts, mother still exists. Even when everything else doesn't. Now, mother, tell me how and I will court jaundice like you once did. My father is a photograph. My mother a photographer. Now, there is a third one.

She wafts in and out of sleep. I want to believe that the sleep is painless but I think not. We talk like each other. We look like each other. We don't think like each other. Now she is calling, the woman my mother dislikes. I must talk to her, my wife, Geeta.

19

Ajit: Making Cake

She wants mangoes. She gave me cake when I wanted it. Maya was three. Mr Swayam was gone for a long time on the road. It was just the three of us.

I volunteered mother for a school event. My mother will make cakes, I had said, little knowing that my mother was working on the biggest project of her life. She would call the project, *Intention: the exhibit.*

When I reached home from middle school I found mother painting, a sign that she was deep in work, painting roguish monkeys—pink faces, blue bodies, orange smiles. She paints when her photographs and writings fail her. She's not bad, she's not spectacular. This is the only place she does not try.

I tell her I have volunteered her to make large cakes, despite her busy schedule. She opens her mouth to say something, then waves her hand in front of her face.

"Sure, Ajit, I will make the cakes first."

The cakes were waiting for me at the dining table when I came back from school the following week. The next weekend she got jaundice and stayed sick with yellow pupils for over a month.

Mother gave me cakes when I asked for it, why cannot I bring her mangoes when she needs them?

Mother is the fountain, *phuvara* of love that falls down from all sides.

Somewhere in between these crumpled sheets and heavy quilts, mother is there. And this will.

I'm sorry, mother. I cannot send you away happy. Maya and I have something in common. Something other than mother. A brother. A love for Mr Swayam. And now a regret at having failed our best friend.

✳ ✳ ✳

20

Jon

Ajit says that Maya wants me to have the camera.

"Are you sure," I asked him. He nods.

"Why don't we ask Suchitra if it's okay?" I suggest.

"She doesn't care about anything anymore," Ajit says. Except one thing. And then we both fall silent.

They are all sad, yet I can feel a sense of peace, a happiness bubbling up inside me. They are sad because they love her and she is leaving. She is leaving with her deepest wish unfulfilled. I'm happy because I have finally found someone. I know that she is leaving, yet my heart is not breaking, not aching. Am I ahead of the curve or behind? Will it ache after she is snatched away? Suchitra has made happiness sexy for me. There are many that don't wish you to come to harm. A friend is someone who does something about it. She is my someone.

And yet the shadows return at the slightest whiff of memory. *How can I be with a man who has checked out from his own life?* Yes, how can she? How can anyone? Will I forever be the man who has checked out from his life?

"Why do you love this camera so much?" I asked her the first week.

"This camera is the reason I found you."

And my camera is the reason I found her.

Secrets are told to those who can keep a secret. Today she told me a secret.

What can you get from an old girl? she'd asked me the first day. What can you get from an old girl? The real thing.

21

Ram Sharan

My father, Sahib Ram, he is dying with Suchitra. I can see that. That anger. His anger is gone. He is feebler, humbler. Death will be final. You never see that person again. Nothing crushes hope like it. We don't have the mangoes. She will leave. He will have nothing. He will have no hope. What is the antidote to wishing? To hoping? *You look like a Sahib, Sahib Ram,* she had said to him the first week. *Yes, finally, Babyji.*

What birth could not fulfill for Sahib Ram, life eventually brought to him, my father. She told Jon a secret today. She stopped me when I was about to leave the room. Then she asked Jon to leave, said to me, "What a lucky man Sahib Ram is to have a son like you. I will tell your mother this when I meet her."

Why am I crying? Crying for this woman? Crying for myself? In these weeks I have discovered my own secret. Pain is not a punishment. Just like happiness is not a reward.

✳ ✳ ✳

22

Suchitra

How do you tell someone the story of your life? Where do you start? What do you omit? What do you highlight? If it is a young person, do you lie, do you say yes, it will all work out in the end? That what you've lost is not important? The experience will stand you in good stead? Do you lie or speak the truth? Take them behind the curtain and show them that doing your duty is no reward. It is simply a shoe that fits better. Yes, you must lie. You must tell them there is nothing to fear. And then tell them the truth. What is the truth? Your word is the truth.

This boy thinks he has come to me for himself. No. He has come to me for me. Just like Ajit sent Daddyji and Bui happy from the world, he is here to remind me that everything was not for nothing. I want to tell him that when you live the life that has been chosen for you, you can choose how you will die. But that is not the secret that he is ready to hear. He is not here to learn how to die.

They say it is not possible. That I must settle.

This boy is my witness. Perhaps I was wrong in all that I said to Jon. Maybe it will not work out. Maybe he's just here to see what to do when things don't work out. "But..." Ajit said, "...I understand, mother, but we must be practical." It was the first time in his life I have heard the words but and Ajit next to each other. Mangoes are mangoes and apples are apples. Why should I be pragmatic?

Sahib Ram asks me at least once each day: *How do you feel, Babyji?* How do I feel? So much conversation. So many words, and still not enough said.

My trinity: my Swayam, my John Papi, my Sahib Ram. Together we have eaten so many things.

Swayam and I, so many rides, airplanes, dreams, so much humiliation, so much pain, so much restlessness. With Sahib Ram I have eaten ice pops in the winter, mangoes in the summer, thrown pebbles in the river, together we ate away at each other's loneliness, at our emptiness that is ever ready to enter our homes like an unannounced guest.

My heart is light. I have shed all that was not mine. It has been cleaned of anger and hate.

I'm a lucky girl to have so much company near my end. Only my girls are missing for it to be perfect. The mangoes. They stress too much about it. I know my monkeys will get their mangoes.

Jon tells me that the monkeys have company. Squirrels. Many, many squirrels. It's always good to have company. And then when you have company, you must have food. Something sweet. Something sour.

I tell Jon what Swayam had once told me, "When you sit in attendance of the moment, the photograph will come. The camera is just a device. You create the photograph. You will it there with your determination. It takes courage to get naked. It takes love to get naked in front of someone willingly. It takes courage to get naked in front of yourself."

So long this waiting. Now we will meet in the big ocean. From this cold, the body will soon become warm, uncomfortably warm. My monkeys. My monkeys will get their mangoes. My heart; love is the sweetest mango. Nanga Baba was right.

Everything that is false will have the opportunity to become true. Oh God, Mr Peeko, I know where Mr Peeko was born.

"The steps small, the breath short; it's just like a hike, Sahib Ram," I say.

23

Release

Ajit had just turned in when his cell phone rang. He heard Geeta say hello and then his phone died. His global phone didn't work the way it is supposed to work. Less than two minutes later the landline across the hallway rang. The same instrument on which Sahib Ram had heard Suchitra tell him that she was *coming home*. Ajit ran towards this receiver in the darkness and hit his knee against the side table.

"Hello?" he groaned.

"Honey, are you ok?"

"Geeta…"

Ajit took a deep breath. "Yeah, it's fine. It'll be fine." He massaged his knee and found a place to sit down in the darkness. "She's been asking for both of you, when are you and Maya…"

Geeta cuts him short. They patch in Maya and resume the conversation.

"We're coming, Ajit, but first…it's about the mangoes. Ajit…I think we have something."

She told him how she'd been crying in the break room. A new intern saw her as she wiped her face.

"How can I help…?"

"I don't think you can," says Geeta unwilling to be drawn into the conversation.

But this young woman persisted. For almost five minutes after the narration, the intern, Asmita, cupped her hands over the mouth and swayed from side to side. Then she started a pot of coffee and said something to Geeta that would lift a lot more than her mood.

"You must listen to me very carefully, Geeta. I have an Uncle," Asmita said tentatively.

"The gentleman who dropped you off on the first day to work…" Geeta nodded. "Yes, I know."

"No, not him. This one is my mother's brother. He is the black sheep of my mother's family. Or least used to be. Until he made good—with his knowledge of some things."

"What things?" said Geeta.

When they are done talking, Geeta laughs, cries, remembers something her mother-in-law had said to her in the first year of her marriage.

It is such an extraordinary story and Geeta narrates it with excruciating precision for the brother-sister duo.

There was silence at the other end for a little bit and Geeta waited for Ajit to take in the news and respond with an exclamation of joy or relief or something in between.

But all he could bring himself to say was, "Are they good mangoes, Geeta?"

"Really, Ajit, every time I forget that you are your mother's son, you remind me," she says, half amused.

Maya remains quiet. Listening.

Today Geeta leaves their three-way call before Maya, so that the brother and sister can have a quiet word with each other.

✳

It appeared so simple and easy once it was settled. Yes, of course, genetically engineered mangoes that develop at the slightest trace of sunlight—just an hour away from Kalka, closer to Delhi, grown in a farm house, the weekend home of a closeted food scientist. The plains were getting primed for the summer. But Ajit wondered if this good luck would last. He did not tell her about it. He did not want her last feeling to be that of disappointment. Plus, she would have probably said something like, *kairi to nahin hai?* That part he'd taken care of when he asked Geeta if they were good mangoes.

✳ ✳ ✳

24

Reading

There is no need for anyone to know which year this might be, there is no other moment but this. The room is warm, so warm that it is easy to forget that just over an hour and half ago, it would have been hard to sit in it without wrapping oneself in three layers and a thick blanket. A few wooden chips and Sahib Ram's blackened hands have changed all that.

But Suchitra, newly sixteen, is still not very friendly with gratitude.

"Babyji, the fire is ready," and Babyji is ready too, with wet hair to soak the warmth of that fire. Suchitra likes to read aloud and Sahib Ram likes to hear the sound of her voice. "Sahib Ram, can you hurry, please! I really would like to get started..."

She is always impatient. He is always patient with her. Not always patient. There is no human being like that. Or is there?

Sahib Ram is wearing brand new trousers,

cotton blended with just little silk, a white shirt and a golden-rust cardigan. The trousers and cardigan are Daddyji's, Bui has had them altered for Sahib Ram. The shirt is a present from Suchitra, fresh and clean, bought from the Sunday market in the lower bazaars, a market that becomes a home for hand-me-downs on Sunday mornings, and yet there is one vendor who sits there every Sunday and sells brand new khadi cotton skirts—white and grey. Nothing else. This vendor, a man in a kangra cap smiles when Suchitra asks him if the fabric is unblemished. He reassures her that it is unwashed, untouched. Newly hand spun.

Together they read. The story is in English and Sahib Ram understands English, but Suchitra translates anyway. She likes the practice. She can think in two languages, but they are different kinds of thoughts. She wants to squeeze this gap. Make one language a lover of the other. She reads, recites. In between, she pauses.

"What do you think, Sahib Ram?"

Sahib Ram has taken off his vest. "I'm dying in this heat, Babyji."

Suchitra ignores Sahib Ram's last comment. She likes the room to be toasty. She wants to be angry, but except once, she has never been angry with Sahib Ram. Today will not be that first time.

A little farther away from them, on the ottoman, sleeps a black corduroy jacket that Suchitra has bought for Sahib Ram. A gift on his last birthday. This is the jacket Sahib Ram will burn the day Suchitra sails for London.

"Let's underline all the new words," she says.

The pencil is blunt. Again, it will be Sahib Ram who will fetch his half-sawed razor blade and deftly slice through the wooden cylinder to shave brown pencil skin and leave the black graphite shiny, ready to write.

"No, I need it to be more pointy," Suchitra says.

So Sahib Ram, Suchitra's lover, her sibling, goes at it again. They can read each other. But still they must read together. When they are done reading, Suchitra announces grandly to Sahib Ram, like she has heard the radio host announce at the end of the dramtised play.

"Yeh kahani ab poorn roop se samaapt hui."

❊

Suchitra is sleeping. Really sleeping. Not dead. When she wakes, she finds Sahib Ram in her room. No Ajit, Jon, Ram Sharan or Meena.

Sahib Ram sits in Ajit's chair today. He does not know it, but he is crying. But of course, he knows it. His face is wet. Suchitra wakes up.

"How does it feel, Babyji?"

Suchitra swallows for a few minutes.

"Just like a hike, Sahib Ram." Then suddenly, she is chatty. "What should I tell everyone, Sahib Ram? What should I say that you said?"

"Say that I said thank you, Babyji."

"Not dhaanyavad, Sahib Ram?" There is a faint trace of a giggle.

"No Babyji, no dhaanyavad for me now. I am a Sahib, so I say thank you. *Thank you ji!"*

They laugh. Sahib Ram his loud laugh and

Suchitra, hers punctured by coughs.

"Yes, Sahib Ram, I will tell everyone there, 'Thank you for the love. Sorry for the fights.' You tell everyone here and I will tell everyone there."

They fall quiet. In this room where they have read so many stories together.

Suchitra speaks again for the two of them. "Sahib Ram, Yeh kahani ab poorn roop se samaapt hui." She swallows again many times before she can find the strength to translate, "Sahib Ram, this story is now officially over."

Sahib Ram, his tears, they will not be contained now. His story, it is over too.

25

Waiting

It's still 1938. It's a long year. Sometimes so much happens in one year, the other years sort of compress to compensate. Sahib Ram wished he could put his heart in hibernation. He saw the squirrels run away, not to be seen for months. He wished he could run away somewhere. Mostly he wished he could find a place in this world where he would be free of himself. Sahib Ram wished and wished and wished and then one day he got his wish. The heart, it went in hibernation. And it stayed that way up until a long time.

But now, all this waiting through the seasons, waiting for the mangoes has done something to him. Every injection that is administered surreptitiously to Suchitra does something to him. He is beginning to fear for his heart. Perhaps the season of hibernation is over but it's not summer yet. And it's all her fault. This girl he has seen in pyjamas, in patialas, in saris, once in bell bottoms and now in this maxi hospital gown. This girl, once young, now old, his girl, eternal girl.

The aeroplane did not land smoothly. Smita Garewal, a petite woman with a fondness for makeup and sweaters with big buttons with embroidery on the shoulders did not open her eyes till they landed. She had done this ride several times before and was still not accustomed to the bumpiness of the ride; it was not gentle like the bumpiness of a train.

Aeroplanes don't swoop down elegantly like eagles. This was the only time she begrudged herself and her husband their new-found wealth. The other times she could bring herself to appreciate the side effects of wealth.

Ajit was waiting for her when the plane landed. Mrs Garewal turned out to be a petite woman who was more than happy to bring the mangoes to Suchitra. The crate of mangoes was not really a crate. They came neatly packed in a green plastic cylinder. He counted them, there were three cylinders and one bonus. Bonus for a dying woman. Genetically engineered mangoes.

"My husband hopes that Sunrise Mangoes will become a household name soon." Ajit wants to nod, to say something in appreciation, to second her wish but he opts for quiet.

Ram Sharan drove him back as fast as he could along the single lane winding road. They exchange glances with each other. Every once in a while, they would cross a truck driver, more impatient then them and Ram Sharan would have to accede.

Suchitra was asleep when they arrived. But for all his rushing, Ajit did not know what to do once they reached home. As Ali, the driver of the vehicle carrying the mangoes, moved ahead to thrust the crates inside the room, all the men—Ajit, Ali, Jon, Sahib Ram and the doctor—stood soberly at the sight of the mangoes: soft, yellow not quite orange or plush, but still plump with juice and promise. Only Meena knows what to do. She opened the crate, creating as much noise as she could. Suchitra's eyelids wrinkled ever so slightly, roused by the sound.

Meena took the crate of mangoes to Suchitra and had her place her hand on the mangoes as a benediction.

"What are you waiting for, mother? What are you waiting for, mother? The mangoes are here. They are here. Go light," said Ajit exultantly.

26
Flight

It was Sahib Ram who did the honors. Ajit and all the others were busy with the cremation. It was a cold day, colder than usual.

"Aaao, aaao, baccha. Aacha baccha..." he tried to coax the monkeys out of their reticence.

"I've never seen a monkey responding to aacha baccha," Jon said trying to settle his tripod over the best condition he could find over the uneven ground. His knowledge of Hindi had improved dramatically in the past several weeks.

Sahib Ram silenced him with a wave of the hand.

"Any animal will respond to anything a child responds to."

They stood there for a while. The mangoes lay in the centre, on a jute *chatai,* a mat, some cut open with a knife, others whole. The eviscerated mangoes—their innards are a tantalizing, reddish yellow. The others are round, oval and untouched. But the monkeys are not impressed.

"Maybe we should leave them to it," said Jon.

"No, they worry that it might be a trick. All these mangoes..."

Sahib Ram would not leave until he saw them eating the mangoes for himself. He was not much for privacy during food consumption. But when nothing changed for a long time, Sahib Ram turned to go. He needed a break. His back was getting stiff. Jon took the cover off the lens of Suchitra's favorite camera, now his camera. This was going to be his last day in Shimla. He couldn't live without her here. He must take all the pictures he can. He starts taking pictures, the camera slow. He is a digital guy. But he doesn't mind. He no longer worries about whether they will come out right. The eagle is soon going to be above them, but not yet.

His clicking loosens up the monkeys. Him and his camera they trust. The baby monkey, the one that was small, baby and tasty, comes forward, full of trust. He will try those mangoes. Before the others can stop him, he is eating them and then the other monkeys will realize what fools they have been to mistrust. These mangoes, these mangoes are for them.

Jon calls for Sahib Ram. "Mr Sahib Ram! Sir, Sir!"

Sahib Ram returns.

It has taken a long time to get these monkeys their mangoes. It has required that a human heart be scrubbed clean of anger and hate. Sahib Ram walks around the monkeys and mutters what Suchitra has asked him to say to them, "Thank you for the love. Sorry for the fights. Sorry. Sorry." He will say it twice before he starts crying.

Jon is surprised at how much they ate the mangoes like he might have. The first few mangoes, the skin they tore off, the mango slices they eat them elegantly, almost like ladies.

Just then the eagle swoops in, his entry dramatic as always. But this time the monkeys are prepared. They band together, the baby monkey in their center. They caw caw, moving but stable, ready to die, ready to be mauled. The baby is hidden in the circle, cannot be seen. He's too much work. The eagle flies away. Will he return? Perhaps. For another baby maybe. This one has too many protectors. Protectors who love it. Protectors who have just eaten mangoes.

✳

Tonight, Jon will fly out. Back home. The camera Suchitra gave him, he packs first. He has a roll from this camera ready to be developed. He looks through the images in his digital camera and zooms in on the last picture that he took of Suchitra. She is awake, not yet asleep. But her eyes are closed. Ajit will tell her that the mangoes are here. Meena will repeat after him. Jon will take a picture because he knows what is coming. He has learnt to sit in attendance. A tear rolls down Suchitra's left eye. Suchitra is crying. And yes, she's never looked this beautiful in her life.

✳ ✳ ✳

Acknowledgements

I would like to thank the Fremont Main Library, Fremont, California and the Mahila Mahavidyalaya, Jodhpur, Rajasthan. Also, thanks to Tom Andes for an insightful first read.

I would like to appreciate my team at Leadstart publishing: Malini Nair, Naina Solanki, Kavya Shree, Rajesh Bale, for all their hard work and dedication. Finally, I would like to thank my family for continuing support.